Picture a Girl

JENNY MANZER

Picture a Girl

ORCA BOOK PUBLISHERS

Copyright © Jenny Manzer 2024

Published in Canada and the United States in 2024 by Orca Book Publishers.
orcabook.com

All rights are reserved, including those for text and data mining, AI training and similar technologies. No part of this publication may be reproduced or transmitted in any form or by any means, electronic or mechanical, including photocopying, recording or by any information storage and retrieval system now known or to be invented, without permission in writing from the publisher. The publisher expressly prohibits the use of this work in connection with the development of any software program, including, without limitation, training a machine learning or generative artificial intelligence (AI) system.

Library and Archives Canada Cataloguing in Publication
Title: Picture a girl / Jenny Manzer.
Names: Manzer, Jenny, author.
Identifiers: Canadiana (print) 20230466524 | Canadiana (ebook) 20230466532 |
ISBN 9781459836662 (softcover) |
ISBN 9781459836679 (PDF) | ISBN 9781459836686 (EPUB)
Subjects: LCGFT: Novels.
Classification: LCC PS8626.A6792 P53 2024 | DDC jC813/.6—dc23

Library of Congress Control Number: 2023941297

Summary: In this middle-grade novel, Addie has to draw on all her resilience to look after herself and her little brother, Billy, when their mother, who struggles with depression and alcoholism, leaves unexpectedly.

Orca Book Publishers is committed to reducing the consumption of nonrenewable resources in the production of our books. We make every effort to use materials that support a sustainable future.

Orca Book Publishers gratefully acknowledges the support for its publishing programs provided by the following agencies: the Government of Canada, the Canada Council for the Arts and the Province of British Columbia through the BC Arts Council and the Book Publishing Tax Credit.

Cover artwork by Sophie Dubé
Interior art by SirenaArt / Creative Market
Design by Rachel Page
Edited by Sarah Howden
Author photo by Hélene Cyr

Printed and bound in Canada.

27 26 25 24 • 1 2 3 4

*To A.J., Briar and David—
who all love a stormy day by
the ocean and a good story.*

Sometimes a story is all you have left.

SUNDAY

When Mama is happy, there is no one who shines brighter. Her eyes sparkle like beach glass, and she makes this snorting sound just before she laughs. Every night before we turn out all the lights in the cabin, she tells us a story. The story could be about me and my brother, Billy, though it's often about some adventure in Mama's life. It's important to listen carefully and not to make assumptions, Mama says.

For example, you might assume that Billy's name is William, but the name on his birth certificate, for real, is Billabong, after the surf brand.

Billabong is also a word from Australia, a place I dream of visiting, where it is almost always hot and there are kangaroos, koalas and spiders and plants that can kill you—and friendly people who say "G'day." Maybe the spiders and plants don't mean to kill—they just have a poison inside that gets released when they're scared.

When Mama's home, night is my favorite time in the cabin. The dark falls and its edges soften. You can't see the mold around the corner of the windows, and if all three of us are here, it feels safe. Sometimes the rain starts up, and we can hear it tapping like impatient fingers on the cedar-shake roof. I lie in my bed listening to the waves crashing and Billy snoring.

Sometimes when Mama gets angry, she points to the ceiling of the cabin and shouts, "You'll do what I say under my roof!" And then she shakes her hands, like she's releasing water droplets from them. What she doesn't say is that it's not really her cabin. It belongs to Mr. Chadawack, or Mr. Chadawacky, as we call him when he's not in earshot. He's got a big red face and a scrubby silver beard and a large belly. He wears beige shorts with lots of pockets and thick flannel shirts. Mama pays him a fortune for our tiny cabin, known as number 32. We like to call it the Storybook Cabin. A creek named Stonybrook runs nearby, but when Billy was littler he called it Storybook, and the name stuck.

Something else you should know: we live exactly fourteen paces from the Pacific Ocean, near Aerie Beach. It's off Better's Bay in the town of Cedarveil. The bay is not called that because it's better, but because someone lost a bet playing cards years ago, and it cost them their fishing boat. I like to know the stories behind things. I save stories the way the tooth fairy collects teeth, Mama says. Mama is really good at two things (three if you count making French toast): surfing and telling stories.

It's Sunday afternoon, so we do what we always do: (1) cabin chores, (2) pack our school lunches and (3) leave Mama in peace and quiet so she can gather her thoughts. Mama has these moods, which she says she inherited from her mother. When she is in them, look out. Most of the time, Mama is a monarch butterfly, bright and black at once, flitting from job to job. When she is in a mood, she becomes that same butterfly pinned to a board, silent and still. It's best to leave her alone.

"Billy," I say. "Fill up the lamp and sweep the floors, okay?" He is lying on his stomach across our crocheted circle rug, reading some garage-sale

X-Men comics. Billy has a lazy streak, and he needs someone like me to remind him what to do. When I was his age, I filled the lamps all the time. We have electricity in the cabin, but it sometimes gets knocked out, so we have to be prepared.

"Why do I have to?" he whines, staring at me with his big brown eyes. Billy is a good-looking kid and smart too. Everyone says so, like the cashier at the Save Easy or Martin Daley, the guy who runs the So Clean Laundromat with his wife, Lila. He plays bass in the local roots-rock band, and Lila gives Billy and me milky tea with sugar and digestive biscuits or even homemade fritters because we help our mother so much.

"Shush up, you two," shouts Mama from where she lies on her bed. "Mama has a headache from all your shouting," she adds, even though she was the only one shouting.

I know what's coming next. She's going to need her "medicine," as she calls it, to soothe her headache and her jitters. She peeks over a quilt, looking irritated, her blue eyes fixed on me. Her hair was neatly done in two braids this morning, but now tendrils and strands are poking out. She's shivering because she's still wearing a T-shirt that says *Eat. Sleep. Surf.* and denim cutoffs. Her favorite thing to wear is a wetsuit, and the salty smell of neoprene always makes me think of her. Watching my mom carve a wave on her shortboard is like watching LeBron play basketball—which I sometimes do at other kids' houses. (We don't have a TV.) She's never had any coaching or training. She was just born to surf.

"Billy, bring me my medicine," she says. I don't like how she gets when she drinks that stuff, but I don't like how she gets without it either. The bottle is in the top cupboard, above the kitchen sink, so Billy has to drag a chair over. The wood cabinets are breaking down from the damp air in the cabin, and little chips of wood flake off every time we open the cupboards. They were once painted bright green, like the kitchen table.

"Thank you, lovey," she says, her mood shifting in a finger snap. Without being asked, Billy brings her the gold-rimmed teacup she likes. It has orange and pink flowers wound around it and once belonged to Mama's grandmother—supposedly the only posh thing she owned.

"Finish the sweeping, Billy," I remind him. If we play our cards right, we'll be free to roam the beach—and still get story time, the best part of the day. The key is that Mama has enough of the drink to make her happy but not so much that she falls asleep. She started taking it almost every night two years ago, after she hurt her back while unloading bags of flour during a shift at the café. First she took these pain pills for a few weeks, but then the doctor wouldn't renew her prescription. She was so mopey when her back hurt because she couldn't surf. Might as well have cut off her oxygen, she said.

I rummage around our kitchen cupboards to see what there is to make our school lunches. The possibilities include oatmeal, a jar of olives, a tin can of maple syrup, two cans of black beans, a sack of whole-wheat flour and a bag of brown rice. The fruit bowl on the counter holds two red apples and three ripe bananas. I press my finger against a spot on the banana. Brown bananas are as bad a lunch as stinky tuna. It would be better to starve than to pack those. My name, Adelaide Scratch, is strange enough, not to mention my too-long bangs, my too-tall body and the fact that my toes poke out of my runners.

Billy sweeps halfheartedly, gripping the broom like a hockey stick. He glances over at his lunch kit, which I have placed on the table. It doesn't go well when we leave lunches to the morning. None of us like getting up early unless it's to go surfing. Surfing is the reason Mama moved to Aerie Beach four years ago, when I was seven and Billy was four.

Mama works, for sure, just not every day. Cedarveil is a summer tourist hub on the southwest side of Vancouver Island. We have lots of people here who work around the clock in summer and can't find a job in winter. Mama is somewhere in between. If she surfs all the time, we run out of money and our lights get turned off. I can't wait until I put together enough money to take the Red Cross babysitting course. It costs seventy dollars for two days, and after I pass I can legit make money for myself. That will be the best.

"I can't wait to babysit," I say to Billy, keeping my voice low. I've found a jar of unopened pea butter in the back of the cupboard. It's not my favorite, but it's a strong candidate to star in tomorrow's lunch.

"Why? You always complain when you hafta watch me."

"I don't get paid to watch you. Plus, when you babysit you get to see other people's houses, like if they have big-screen TVs, or what kind of books they read, whether they have a garburator."

"A what?" he asks.

"It's this thing that blends your garbage," I say.

"Like making a smoothie?"

"Gross! No. It makes your garbage smaller—like, liquefies it."

"That's why you want to babysit?"

"Of course not. I like little kids," I say. I don't want to tell him that I like to imagine having baths in other people's tubs or filling a glass with ice from a machine that spits out cubes. We only have a stall shower, Band-Aid beige, and a fridge so old that it hums like a power line every night. I am curious about how other people live. When I ride my ridiculously pink bike around Cedarveil in the evening, I always want to peer in and see what people are doing behind their curtains.

Sundays, Billy and I might go to the beach to collect beer and pop cans to return, gather seaweed to dry or play Frisbee—but I hear rain starting up. Mama takes a deep sip from her teacup. Her drink smells awful to me—a mix of cinnamon and turpentine. But it eases whatever was itching Mama, and she rises to the stove. I watch her bustle around the galley kitchen, opening and shutting drawers and cupboards. She finds a bunch of leeks from the farmers' market in the fridge and holds them up. The leeks are wilted, their limp stalks drooping.

"Still good," she says, tossing the bunch onto a wooden cutting board. She chops quickly, as if on high speed. Mama is a whiz in the kitchen, the slicing and dicing, which is why she usually picks up work doing prep at resorts or cafés. People can't help but like Mama, and she gets lots of second chances. It doesn't hurt that she's so pretty, with her deep-set eyes and upturned freckled nose—often covered in sunblock if she's surfing. Plus, if you ever need to move, Mama shows up to help—if she remembers.

I watch her locate a brown paper bag of potatoes with long white tentacles stretching out the top. She quickly chops the tentacles off, her knife slicing into the pale, yellow flesh. By the time Billy is done sweeping and has started his school reading, she's made a potful of leek and potato soup. On the very best nights, she sometimes makes homemade bread as well. But tonight it is just the steaming soup.

We settle around the green table, our spoons clinking in the same rhythm as we eat. I watch her teacup, checking to see if she's refilling it. She gets annoyed if she notices I'm watching how much she pours, so I just use furtive little fish eyes.

"I heard talk there's some new surf contest starting up here," says Mama, stirring her soup around and around so it makes little whirlpools. "One for girls and women, or something. Cash prize to the winners."

"Is that so?" Billy asks, because it's a good thing to say if you want Mama to keep talking.

"I'll bet you'd win it, Mama. You should enter," I say, almost halfway done my soup already. I must be growing again. I've got a badger digging holes in my stomach, Mama says. She tells me I'm a natural surfer, but I lack finesse, which is another way of saying I lack skill. So I keep waiting until she has time to help me get more finesse, like her. I just need more practice.

"I'm too old for that now," Mama says in a sad tone.

"No you're not, Mama," says Billy, not sucking up but genuine. "You're the best surfer I've ever seen. For a real-life person, like, not on YouTube." Billy almost never lies to Mama. He has been known to fudge the truth with others, however. He's also addicted to YouTube videos, but he can only see them at school or at a friend's house.

"Thanks, sweet pea," says Mama gruffly, swiping her bowl off the table. She's blinking while she runs water to wash dishes at the kitchen sink with the dripping tap, and I know she is sad and touched by what Billy has said—even though it's the truth. Watching Mama surf is like watching a heron take off and glide, especially if she catches a six-foot wave.

Mama switches on our old radio, and we listen to a show about books. I like the soothing sound of the announcer's voice as she asks questions. The writer is French Canadian, I can tell by her accent, and she usually writes for adults, but she has just published a children's fantasy book called *Caspian's Way*.

"*So, did you always want to be a writer?*" the announcer asks.

"*Not at all,*" the author answers. "*I never even considered it. The only book we had in the house was the Bible. My parents wanted me to be a dentist—a steady, useful job. But the stories were circling around my head like sharks. They wouldn't let me sleep.*"

Like sharks, I think, imagining their beady eyes and bodies like gray submarines. I make a note to ask my English teacher, Ms. Cranberg, about *Caspian's Way*. I love lying on my bed and reading and listening to the rain. Cedarveil gets a hundred feet of rain every year, and sometimes in winter I think we'll never see the sun. But winter brings the best waves for surfing, so it's a silver lining. Someday I want to be as good as Mama at duck diving into the waves, waiting for the right one, a real bomb. That means a big wave, in surf talk. I've been skipping rope on the patch of gravel by the side of our cabin and doing push-ups on our carpet because I read these exercises will make my surfing better.

Finally, when we are ready for bed, Mama lies down and pats the space on either side of her. "Okay, groms," she says. That's short for grommets, or young surfers. It's her nickname for both of us when we're all together. It's time for a story. Mama clears her throat and begins.

HEY, RAYLENE!

"Picture a perfect early-summer day in Cedarveil, with a warm Pacific breeze and the sun illuminating the kelp draped over the beach, like Rapunzel's hair but green."

She waited while we pictured.

"You know I've had a lot of really wild things happen while I'm surfing. There was the time the orca surfaced next to me, so close I could smell its briny breath—and I nearly got sliced in two by its dorsal fin.

"I've salvaged a lot of things too. Once a plastic-wrapped box containing the board game Risk washed ashore. I've found an almost-new Swiss Army knife, a Hulk frisbee and a mask and snorkel, because the sea provides. But that particular summer's day, I was lying on my board, waiting for the right wave. I rode one in, just like any other, but when I came to shore, I noticed something bobbing in the water. It looked like a white rope. But it wasn't a rope at all—it was a ribbon. And attached to that ribbon was a bright turquoise box.

"I sat cross-legged in my wetsuit and placed the box on my lap to inspect it. It was a small, wet perfect box with the words *Tiffany & Co.* written on it. I held my breath for a second. It looked special. I opened the box, and sure enough, there was a square diamond ring sparkling in the sunshine, almost as if it winked at me. I couldn't believe it.

"All kinds of possibilities rushed to my brain. Had the box fallen from a cruise ship? Or maybe someone had thrown the engagement ring in the ocean after their beloved said no to their marriage proposal? I knew I couldn't keep it—it didn't belong to me. When I took a closer look, I realized it was engraved. *To Raylene, light of my life. Please say YES.*

"So I stashed the box in my backpack, tucked my surfboard under my arm and decided to search the beach to see if anyone looked like Raylene. There was a family of five, including twin toddlers, seniors taking photos, teens playing a game of Ultimate Frisbee in between the driftwood logs—and some shubies."

The term *shubies* comes from seeing people who wear shoes to the beach. It refers to people who put on flashy surf gear but don't really surf. Mama has no time for shubies taking up space on her beach. Maybe slightly worse is a benny, which is what Mama calls visitors who crowd her out of her favorite surf spots.

"But you kept trying," prompts Billy.

"I did," says Mama, with a grin. "And sure enough, at the end of the beach was a young couple lying next to a fancy wicker picnic basket. They'd fallen asleep, side by side. She was wearing this beautiful lemon-yellow sundress, and he was in Hawaiian-print swim trunks. They hadn't noticed the tide was coming up. So I bent down and did the only thing I could do."

She pauses here. Billy and I know all her stories, but sometimes she changes little details if the mood strikes her.

"I screamed, 'HEY, RAYLENE!' and the woman shot forward like I'd touched her with a hot poker. Oh, Lord, did she jump.

"'What's going on?'" asked the man, who had an English accent, rubbing his eyes. Turned out they had flown over just the day before and were suffering from jet lag something fierce.

"'How did you know my name?' asked the woman, Raylene.

"'I think it's going to be a day of surprises,' I said to Raylene, then asked the man if I could have a word with him. He became fully alert then and began frantically searching the sand for the Tiffany's box. His head was pivoting around here and there, just like a barred owl's."

I wanted to hear more about the diamond. I wanted to know what it felt like to hold something expensive, made just to be beautiful. I wish my mother had tried it on. I used the internet at school to look up Tiffany's once. Even the empty boxes are expensive. The rings all cost thousands of dollars, more than a used truck.

But I don't want to spoil the moment, when Mama is happy and proud of how she helped the young couple from London, England. I want to swim after it like it's leading me through warm waters to a sunlit cave.

"I passed him the box from behind my back, real cool. The man, Eli, was so grateful, he had tears in his eyes. He dropped on one knee, right in the sand, and asked Raylene to marry him. I heard they celebrated that night with the very best table at Farmer's Garden."

Mama's eyes are shining like she was the one who went to the restaurant, the most expensive place in town, where they charge a lot of money to fancy up the stuff locals eat all the time—garlic scapes and wild mushrooms and salmon and seaweed.

"I saw them both on the beach the next day," she says. "Raylene was all shy and happy, showing me the diamond. And that was the most amazing thing I ever found in the sea."

Billy sighs, content. He reaches over and smooths the side of Mama's hair. My brain is swimming with questions. I want to know why they didn't offer Mama a reward. Isn't that what people do? Mama has a good heart—that's what everyone says.

The truth? I sometimes wish she'd just kept the diamond. It could have bought so much food. It would have meant so many fewer trips to the Food Share office down by the old fish-canning plant. They always give us the same thing: no-name peanut butter, canned beans, a box of macaroni and a tin of peaches. On the other hand, she might have spent it on that stuff she drinks, so maybe we were better off with no reward.

I move to my small single bed, and Billy climbs into his. The only walls in the cabin are in the bathroom. Still, we all somehow manage to keep secrets. I lie in bed thinking about school the next day, about stuff I want to tell my friend Pokey, how I hope Wendy Wishart leaves me alone this week. I worry I am going to stay up all night thinking, but then sleep pulls me down and sweeps me away like a riptide.

MONDAY

When I wake up, I sense a stillness in the cabin, as if the rain made everything heavy and quiet. There is no scent of coffee or toast in the air, no smell of anything except the slight dankness of the cabin that never quite leaves no matter how much we air it out in summer.

"Mama?" I ask. My voice quavers. My words sound like they come from someone slipping slowly on a patch of ice, frightened and wobbly. I dig my nails into my palm to distract myself from the sound of the wind thumping against the side of the cabin.

I know right away that she is gone. Again. Billy is still sleeping, curled up in his bed, a soft mound under the covers. Seeing the slope of his shoulder makes me sad. He is going to be hurt and worried and angry. I look for her beat-up Blundstone boots by the front door, even though I know they are gone. Her green backpack is missing, along with the robin's-egg-blue Helly Hansen rain jacket she wears almost year-round. My eyes adjust to the light, and I blink back tears. I notice a piece of lined paper sitting on the kitchen table. She must have torn it from one of my school notebooks. I frown in annoyance.

Dear Adelaide and Billy,

Gone for a little adventure.

Love you,

Mama

I sigh and bite my lip so hard I get the tinny taste of blood. There's no mention of how long she'll be gone this time. There's a legion of blank lines remaining, yet that's all she thought to say.

I think, as usual, about food. There is never enough. I start throwing open the kitchen cupboards, banging the doors, making noise. Angry. I find a bulk-food bag of steel-cut oats that has enough in it to make two bowls. There's half a carton of milk in the fridge. It's not much, but it's something. I stand over Billy, take a deep breath, knowing in ten seconds his day will be ruined.

"Wake up, Billy," I say, placing my hand on his shoulder and shaking.

He turns his head, squints at me.

"She's gone again, isn't she?"

It's not really a question. He can see it on my face.

I nod. He knows the drill. Up, put on cleanish shirt, eat oatmeal, brush teeth, out. He is ready in eight minutes, albeit still wearing the shorts he slept in. I glance at my watch as I lock the cabin door behind us. It is a misty May morning, and we have both underdressed—but there is no time to change.

"Why does she have to go away?" he asks, kicking a fat pine cone from the path. It hits a tree and pinballs back, ricocheting off his shin. We snort-laugh, despite it all.

"Dunno," I say, because who can answer this but Mama? Maybe even she doesn't know. She needs a break sometimes, she told me once. She has to remember what it is like to be "Jeanie Bean," girl surfer, not a single mom of two who uses a ski glove as a potholder. Sometimes she takes her surfboard, Joan Jett, with her, other times not. Mama always names her surfboards, and she's had J.J. for a few years.

I quickly check the shed. The board is there. But that doesn't always mean she'll be home any sooner.

Pokey is waiting for us at the corner by the Husky gas station, like he always does. When he sees us, he waves and pulls his earbuds out. We've been friends since we sat next to each other in second grade, when my family had just arrived in Cedarveil. I know Pokey will be waiting every morning. There was only one time he wasn't there. It turned out he had strep throat, which he said was wicked painful.

"What's up, Billy?" asks Pokey, raising his fist for a bump.

"Everything's pretty egregious," says Billy, a word he just picked up, maybe from school.

Pokey just nods and doesn't ask for details. We continue walking in silence, then I freeze, as if I'm about to fall into a sinkhole. I notice a poster on one of our community corkboards, which are dotted around town. They're like Cedarveil's fridge doors, where we post news, such as someone is selling a crab trap or Martin Daley's band has a gig at the Watering Can. This one says something different. *Born to Shred?*

Yes, I think. I can still remember the first time I saw my mother surf through a barrel. I was five, and we were on a road trip to San Francisco. It was as amazing to me as someone walking on water. She seemed to be swallowed down the gullet of a wave, then emerged from the ocean with her hair dripping, her skin shining. She scrambled onshore and gave me a big hug, my cheek against her wetsuit. After that I knew I wanted to surf a barrel myself. I had only just begun to learn, but she made it look so magical. When I was finally able to pop up on the board, it was like opening a Christmas present that was just for me.

Billy and Pokey watch me staring. The poster doesn't look new. I don't know how I missed it. After the headline it reads *Enter the Belle of the Board contest for teen girls and women. Find rules and entry forms at McKinley's Surf Shop or online at bellesurf.ca. Cash prizes!*

"This is the one Mama mentioned."

"That's coming up Saturday," says Pokey impatiently. "It's too late."

I don't know if he means there's no time to train for the contest or that we're late for school.

"You can win two hundred bucks!" says Billy, reading the fine print. "That's a lotta Cool Ranch Doritos!"

"It's for women and teenage girls only. You have to be at least thirteen," says Pokey, reading more of the fine print.

I rip the poster from the board, which is, like, one of the worst things you can do in Cedarveil. Maybe even worse than giving a tourist directions to our secret swimming hole.

"Addie, we're going to be late," says Pokey, tugging on the sleeve of my T-shirt, which is navy-and-white-striped and made of buttery-soft cotton. Mama bought it new for my tenth birthday. I wear as many stripes as I can. I am not wild about flowers or polka dots. I like stripes.

"Hey, don't stretch my shirt," I say.

We all start to run without anyone saying anything. We are late again. My library books bump against my back as I run, the sharp corners reminding me that there is something to look forward to at lunch. I keep the poster clutched in my hand.

I wonder if Ms. Cranberg could lend me a book on how to win a surfing competition. I mean, I know how to surf, but I need the mental edge to *win* and get that prize. Ms. Cranberg is by far my favorite teacher at Cedarveil School, and she's also our school librarian. She's helped me search out books about planets and basketball and marine animals. The library is just one good thing about school. It's predictable, too, which I like. But most kids hate school, so I keep my yap shut about how much I love it. Cedarveil only has one school for younger kids—high school is in the next town over—so Billy and I are at the same one for now. It works out.

As we near the school, Wendy Wishart sticks her head out the classroom window, a smug half smile showing me she's enjoying our tardiness.

"Hey look, it's the Scratch kids, late again. They're slow at everything," she shouts.

I hear someone laugh at that, and when I find out who it was, I will get them. Wendy knows Billy has trouble reading, and bringing it up is a low blow, even for her.

"Billy, head to class," I say. Thank goodness his teacher, Ms. Chan, is nice.

Wendy pretends not to notice when I walk into our homeroom.

"Stripes are *sooo* over," she says as I sit down just as the announcements are beginning.

Later my science teacher, Mr. Rylan, catches me glancing at the contest poster instead of reading from our textbook.

"What's so interesting, Adelaide?"

I flutter a sheet of lined paper in my hand. Wendy's desk is right beside mine. Today that's a good thing.

"It's just a note from Wendy, sir. I haven't read it, of course," I say in my most sincere tone. Along with being tall, I have a deeper voice than most kids my age. I've learned to talk like a grown-up when I need to. Wendy stops finger-curling her hair and glares at me.

"Oh, do share with the group," coos Mr. Rylan, as I suspected he would. Everyone knows that Marcia Wishart keeps threatening to send Wendy and her sister, Evie, to a private school. I would say good riddance except that the Wisharts buy the school some extras, like musical instruments and sports uniforms. And I like sunny little Evie.

"How many more hours do I have to endure? Mother says next year I'm going to the private school up by the lake," I say, pretending to read. "These teachers aren't fit to pump our gas—"

"Okay, we get the idea, Adelaide," says Mr. Rylan, flicking his eyes upward like he already has his fill of listening to the Wisharts. "That's enough."

I nod, crumple the blank page of paper and stuff it into my pack along with the poster, which I have memorized. Ages thirteen to sixteen are eligible. First prize, $500; second prize, $100; third prize, $50 gift card to Rip It Surf. First prize would be enough to pay Chadawack a little back rent and get a few groceries. I would simply have to win.

Picture a Girl

Pokey's mom comes to pick him up for an orthodontist appointment, so I have no one to hang out with at lunch. I decide to do something risky. I leave the school grounds, just walk right off without telling anyone, which is totally against the rules. I walk three blocks toward town and saunter into McKinley's Surf Shop—the one popular with tourists, started by two guys from Vancouver. I swing the door open, chiming the bell, stride up to the front counter and nab a form. No one notices or asks why I'm not in school—so I head back. I sit in the corner of the soccer field, holding the stub of a pencil I find on the ground. The day has brightened a bit, and I use my hand to shade my eyes. A group of kids are playing Ultimate Frisbee. Wendy and her friends are gathered in a knot together, on a bench. I am safe to take out the form.

I do the math and write down a birthday that makes me thirteen. I am so freakishly tall—five foot five at my last checkup—that everyone always thinks I am older than eleven. Mama says my dad was tall too and that I got my height early. I wish she would tell me more about him. I don't really remember much. But she doesn't like to talk about him. Mostly I'm okay being tall, but sometimes I wish people would treat me more like a kid, like when I want to pay a child's fare at the movies. Billy is eight, looks eight and has cheeks like fat apricots that make old ladies smile. I try to make sure he can be a kid at least some of the time. If Mama drinks too much, I wake up early to make sure she wasn't sick in the night or didn't get too hot and strip down to her undies. I protect him, I guess.

I don't know any fancy surfing terms or techniques, but I've been able to ride a wave, at least for a few seconds, since I was seven years old. After watching Mama, I became determined to really rip. When I finally did it, I stayed upright and cruised toward shore before plopping off into the foam. The wind had burned my face. Billy had high-fived me. Mama had crushed me to her chest. We'd both been in wetsuits, so perhaps we looked alike.

"That was magic, Adelaide," Mama had said. "You've got the stuff. Just like your dad."

I'd turned away, not wanting my pride to show on my face.

"What did it feel like?" Billy had asked me, his brown eyes searching. His hair was sticking up, having dried all soft and feathery in the sun and wind.

Picture a Girl

"It was like walking into a mirror and out the other side," I'd tried. It had been magical and had also made me feel real—the fact that I could stand on a corridor of water and stay on my feet and not be scared. I couldn't explain all that to him. Billy had stared at me, still waiting. He was only four then, after all.

"It was like eating a lime popsicle on the hottest day of summer," I had added.

He'd nodded briskly. Since he was four, he's fallen asleep to the sound of surf. One day Billy might be better at surfing than me, though I don't ever tell him that. He has no fear at all, which can get you into trouble. Fear is like chili flakes on pizza. A little shake is fine, necessary even, to keep things interesting, but too much overwhelms everything.

I scan the form. It is complete, except for my mother's signature. *Jeanie Scratch*, I write. I drag out the line after the *h*, just like she does. After all this time, I write her name better than she does.

After school is always the hardest time, as I adjust. I remember again that she is not here, that I have to pretend for Billy—and Pokey—that everything is okay. I can't even let Pokey know she's gone. It's too dangerous. He might eventually tell a grown-up, and I can't take that chance. The three of us walk home together, talking about school and basketball (Pokey likes the Lakers) and video games (which Billy and I play at friends' houses). We leave Pokey at the corner by the gas station and continue to the turnoff that leads to the trail to our house. Pokey's house is in a suburb just over the hill, on a street with garages and driveways and yards with trampolines.

"See you tomorrow," I say to Pokey, holding up a fist to bump.

"See you tomorrow, Addie."

Billy and I walk in silence down the lane. First we have to pass all of Chadawack's other rental cabins, nestled together like brown mushrooms, probably all with green kitchen tables like ours because they come furnished. Some of the cabins are empty, since it's May. I feel a stab of jealousy thinking about Pokey's real house, real dinner and real mother waiting for him. His mom, Pauline, is Japanese, and she makes him miso soup when it's cold and rainy. Sometimes, in the evenings, his dad will play basketball with him or throw a baseball. Then I feel bad for wishing I had another family. Billy and I have a real mother. She's just different.

The door sticks as I unlock it, and the cabin smells stale, like earth and banana peels. The breakfast dishes are still on the table, so I clear them away. I want to collapse into a big chair and drink Fanta and read books. Instead I wash the dishes and set out the skillet to make scrambled eggs for dinner, listening to that stupid tap drip over and over. The *blip-blip* sound makes me furious, and I whisk the eggs extra hard.

"I hate eggs," says Billy, eyeing the bowl.

"I don't care," I answer.

Eggs are what we have, and I don't feel like being nice.

"If you do your homework and eat your dinner, I'll tell you a story."

"I don't care," he says, trying to imitate me and irritate me in one go.

But he gets out his books. After dinner, while he reads, I do my push-ups on the carpet. I think of what story to tell him. The burning in my arms and chest reminds me that I am still here, and every day my body can get a little stronger. I am still here. I am still fighting. My mother fought once too.

THE TIME MAMA SAVED CROOKED RED

"Once there was a western red cedar known as Crooked Red, named because its bark was a rich, rusty red and it was slightly crooked. Its upper branches swayed like a long arm about to give someone a hearty slap on the back. It was different from the other trees, kind of funny-looking, but it held magical powers. Crooked Red was a Listening Tree, and that made it special. Children could sit quietly at the base of Crooked Red, inhaling the scent of the forest, and tell it their secrets or sad thoughts. It would absorb their tears right into its roots.

Picture a Girl

"Every time a child shared a story, Crooked Red would grow a little taller and a little more crooked—getting heavier with the burden. Crooked Red heard about girls who cheated on math tests, and parents who were quick to use their fists, and boys who longed to hear the sound of a dad stomping around their kitchen in the morning."

Billy nods here. He always nods at that part.

"Crooked Red sat near the banks of the Storybook Creek, just twenty paces from the cabin that bears its name. So one day Mama passed by Crooked Red while she was on her way home from harvesting clams. Her long braids were swinging, and she was humming a tune and feeling pretty good, noticing how the sunshine bounced off the leaves in the forest. What she saw next nearly stopped her heart. Crooked Red had a big yellow X marked on its chest—or where its chest would be if it were human.

"'No!' she screamed, in a yell loud enough to travel far across the Pacific Ocean. A baker in Japan dropped the two eggs he was holding.

"Mama vowed to return the next morning to find out who had placed the marker, who intended to murder Crooked Red. And return she did."

"She woke up early, leaving us sleeping in the cabin," recites Billy.

"Shh," I say. Telling a story is like baking a cake—you have to pour it into the pan, set the oven, then give it time to rise—that's what Mama says.

"That's right. Mama made sure she was there at first light, and she sat under Crooked Red and waited. She crossed her arms and frowned her face, and she waited. A few minutes later a black truck rumbled up.

"A big man jumped out. He had small, beady eyes and a beach-ball belly, and he said, 'You're going to have to get out of my way. I'm here to cut down this tree.'

"'Then we've got a problem,' Mama said. 'Because I am here to save this tree. This tree has a name and a purpose. It listens to children when they are sad and soaks up their sorrow.'

"Well, the man stomped his steel-toed boots, and he told Mama that he worked for the resort up the way, the one that helicopters in tourists from all over the world and has one-thousand-dollar-a-night hotel rooms.

"'This tree is on private property,' the man said. 'We're building a boardwalk to a hot tub, and this tree has to go. Now get out of the way, lady, or else.'

"That was the wrong thing to say to Mama. 'Or else' is always the wrong thing to say to Mama.

She started screaming and swearing, and another, smaller man came out of the pickup truck, holding his Tim Hortons coffee and wondering what was making the sound like two lynxes fighting.

"The men tried to offer her a free pass to the resort spa, and then they threatened to call the police, but she kept her caboose planted in front of Crooked Red, not budging. The man with the tiny eyes made a big mistake then and bent down to try to lift her out of the way.

"Mama is slender but strong. She kicked her legs and screamed so loud that the sun fell out of the sky and landed, *plop*, in the rainforest, like an egg yolk into a big green bowl. The two men were startled by the sudden curtain of darkness—and also at Mama's yelling.

"'That tree is coming down!' one of the men said.

"'This tree is personal!' shouted Mama. 'This tree is special. Way more special than a hot tub. More special than a hot tub full of yetis and unicorns!'

"That last point made the men ponder, wondering whether yetis wore swimsuits in hot tubs.

"'I'm not going,' Mama said. She sat down and reached into her backpack. The men looked kind of nervous—but all she took out was a green thermos of hot tea, orange pekoe with milk and four tablespoons of sugar. She took three quick sips, like someone drawing breaths, and closed her eyes.

"'Are you falling asleep?' asked the shorter man, who had a squeaky voice.

"'You either have to save this tree or make a world where children don't feel sad. Can you do that?'

"The men just stood there, staring in disbelief. A few droplets sputtered—like applause that meant a standing ovation of rain was coming. Mama had traveled the world surfing, but she was born and raised in the Pacific Northwest. She knew all about rainstorms. She knew she could withstand them, no matter how fierce. The sky opened then like a drain finally unclogged, and down came a deluge that would have driven the fiercest yeti from the hot tub. The men were soon drenched.

"They shivered, their big teeth chattering, and retreated to wait out the storm in the comfort of their truck. They tuned in their country radio station and closed their eyes—what could it hurt? Mama sat under Crooked Red as the dirt turned to mud. Eventually the men dozed off.

"And Mama got up and slipped off home. But first she did one last thing. She stopped by the side of the truck and emptied her sugary hot tea into the gas tank. When the men awakened, they would find that their truck would not work.

"The men would be stranded in the forest and would have to come up with a story of their own. Surely they could not admit to their boss what had happened.

"Maybe it was the way she'd outsmarted them, or maybe the men began to think of times in their childhood that they could have used a listening tree. We don't know what made them change their minds, but the next day the sun was thumbtacked high in the sky, and Crooked Red was still there. The men built a detour around it, and Crooked Red is still there today.

"And that is how Mama saved Crooked Red."

"Tell it again," says Billy.

"It's already late," I say. "You have school tomorrow." I smooth his hair with my palm, the way Mama sometimes does.

"I miss Mama. I wish she didn't have to go away like she does," says Billy, because he reports everything that pops into his head. Sometimes I think his brain is like a big fishnet with a gaping hole in the middle, so all his thoughts spill out.

"Go to sleep, Billabong," I say.

There's something I don't talk about with Billy—what Mama takes at night is not really medicine. The bottle label says *Canadian Rye Whisky* and it smells like burning candles and cloves. I find the empty whisky bottles under the kitchen sink before she takes them away. Whisky makes my mother sleepy and often very, very sad.

So I lie awake, listening to the tap drip, missing Mama and hating Mama at the same time, and all those feelings make a hard, knotted tangle in my chest.

TUESDAY

We sleep late, until 8:05 a.m., so there is no time for breakfast—and we don't have much in the cupboards anyway. I hand Billy a banana and his school bag, which contains a permission slip that I signed for him to go on a class visit to the town library next week. I wipe his face with a smelly dishcloth and push him out the door. The cabin door is sturdy and thick, and I always lock it and check the handle two times. It makes me feel safe. We don't have a lot, but I don't want anyone ransacking our things when we're at school. I blow out all the air in my cheeks and make a wish that Mama will be home when we return.

"Do you think Mama will come home tonight?" Billy asks, stomping along the trail in my old rubber boots. They are red and say *Spider-Man* on them. Billy and I often have the same thought at the same time. It is freakish, like a lightning bolt striking us both.

"Dunno," I say, listening to my shoes squelch in the mud. I don't want to get his hopes up. Sometimes Mama's away for a short time. Sometimes it's a longer time. The trick is not to trip up and tell anyone she's gone. More than once I've had to fudge it and pretend Mama was just up the road doing some weeding or babysitting or filling in at the recycling depot—all things she sometimes does. The trick to a good lie is to keep a sprinkling of truth in there. I frown at a beer-bottle cap on the trail. It's the first sign of the tourists coming. They'll literally invade our backyard, blocking the trailheads to our best swimming holes with their SUVs. I once saw that someone had stuffed an empty Ruffles bag into an old bear den. Like they don't even respect a black bear's bedroom. Pokey calls them "hot-dog water" sometimes, which makes me laugh, even though Cedarveil needs the tourists to keep the town going. Even Mama knows that.

"If it weren't for them, we'd all be eating kelp," Mama has told us more than once. She's ready to skin the tourists when they intrude on her surf spots, but she knows they bring the seasonal work she does—cleaning rooms, clearing tables, bringing plates of hash browns and egg whites. I can't even imagine being rich enough to leave the yolk part of an egg behind.

At lunch Pokey and I usually sit together on a bench at the corner of the field. We read and we talk. Sometimes Pokey might go play soccer with some of the other kids, but mostly we hang out. Billy has a few friends he runs around with, and he has a different lunch time, so I get a break from him.

I generally try to stay in the background at lunch. Even though I am only eleven, I know my family is a little unusual, what with my Australian dad and Mama, who is not like most moms. Billy is too young to clue in that others might think our family is strange—the way we live in a cabin and return bottles when we need food and wear clothes from the St. Vincent de Paul store. Once, on a Sunday morning, I stole a plastic bag of donations that was sitting out in front of the store. I was hoping for some cherry-red high-top Converses, or at least some girl's shorts, but there were just clothes for old ladies, like housecoats printed with peach flowers, so I brought the whole bag back.

Pathetic, isn't it? That's the favorite word of Wendy Wishart, whose name sounds like wind and magic but who's as mean as a splinter. Her hair is a shiny chestnut shade and bounces from her shoulders. If she wears a paisley-print bandanna in her hair to school, all the rest of the sixth-grade girls rush out to buy one.

Today I am reading *The Crossover* by Kwame Alexander. I like the rhymes and the basketball and the way everything's not all perfect in the story. Because stories are not perfect. They don't all have happy endings. Pokey is sitting next to me, pursing his lips and reading an *Avengers* digest. Pokey's full name is Eli Polk, but we all call him Pokey, and he doesn't mind. He's fast on the soccer field but really is kind of pokey and calm, so hanging out with him suits me, especially when I have firecrackers of worry streaking across my brain. I plan to ask Pokey if he wants to start practicing basketball with me at lunch—I am tall but on the clumsy side. Mama says it's just because I got my height early, and I won't be a butterfingers forever. I hope she's right.

Pokey pages through the comic and hums, which I like because it's a happy noise. He has a strawberry-kiwi juice box balanced on his knee. His mom packs one every day, and sometimes he smuggles an extra one for me. I've told him not to ask, not to be *conspicuous*. I glance at my plastic watch, which has Captain Marvel on it, a present from Pokey for my eleventh birthday. We have eight more minutes before the bell. I breathe in the mown-grass smell of the school fields. We don't have this kind of grass around my house, just sword ferns and rotting logs, so the smell means school to me. And I like school, as I've already admitted.

I am trying to devour one last page before the bell rings. Then someone bumps my elbow and the book falls to the ground, right into a puddle. Seeing the book in the oily wet makes me draw in a breath, like someone has thrown a hard pass to my chest. I turn my head and see Wendy, smiling, waiting to see my reaction to her shove. She is wearing new, hot-pink high-tops that somehow have no mud on them, even though we live in a rainforest. Even the mud stays clear of Wendy Wishart. I usually keep a watch out for her, but the book was too good.

"OMG," she says, pointing to my raggedy runners. The toes of my shoes look like an open fish mouth, gaping. I tuck my foot under the bench and grind my bare toe into the gravel, as if the discomfort will quell the shame I feel. Then I am mad at myself for letting her get to me. That what she thinks matters.

"Those shoes are *sooo* pathetic," she says to her BFF, Layna, who wears two ponytails, one erupting from each side of her head. When she nods vigorously, they turn like helicopter blades.

I pick up my book from the puddle, but I can already see it's too late. The book is ruined. I have no money to replace it. Now my library privileges will be cut off. You must bring a book back in the same condition you found it in. The corners of my eyes pinprick with the beginning of tears. I will not cry in front of Wendy, I will not.

"I think the shoes are cool," says Pokey, closing his comic. "I mean, you're wearing torn jeans. Why is that different?"

Pokey doesn't know that girls like Wendy and Layna don't go by logic or rational arguments. I'm the gazelle getting pulled down into the savanna. Wendy finds me almost every lunch. She never forgets about me.

Wendy is wearing those torn jeans with no knees that I know cost seventy dollars at the Seabreeze

Boutique, where all the tourists go. The pockets have *embellishments*, which are tiny little rhinestones. My mom once worked in retail but said she couldn't stand all the snooty tourists demanding this and that and asking for discounts.

"Where's your mom today, Addie?" Wendy asks, though she can't know my mom has disappeared again. Billy is the only one who knows, and he always keeps that secret. I told Billy that social workers will take us away if he tells. He doesn't really understand what a social worker is, but he knows it's something bad.

"Where's *your* mom, today, Wendy? Maybe she's yelling at a crossing guard," suggests Pokey in a pseudo-helpful tone, but his snicker gives him away. Wendy's mom got in hot water last week after nearly ramming our crossing guard, Walt. She apparently thought he was taking too long helping some kindergartners dawdle across the intersection. Marcia Wishart is one of the few people in Cedarveil who are always in a hurry. The Wisharts own a fancy resort called Moon Over Water, and they are constantly in the local paper.

Wendy glares at Pokey while I stare at the ruined book. I try to wipe it on my jean shorts, which just smears the dirt. I could tell Ms. Cranberg that Wendy threw it in a puddle, but Wendy has a rep for being a good girl, and her parents donated all the money for a new school jungle gym last year, which they never let anyone forget.

"Everyone knows your mom spends her checks at the Liquor Depot. Maybe you can return some bottles and buy some new shoes," says Wendy, before turning on her hot-pink heel and marching off. Layna follows, her ponytails swinging and a tight smile on her face.

I can't believe Wendy has said it. The one thing I never wanted said out loud. Well, not the only thing. But a big thing. She's gone too far. She must be seeking revenge for the note thing in class. I blink back tears, and the ground lurches up toward me as if I'm on a carnival ride. My whole body goes weak, and I drop the book again, right in the same puddle. Now it really is my fault. Shame is burning lava in my belly.

What hurts the most about what Wendy said is that it's kind of true.

"Pokey," I say, my voice trembling. "Someday soon I'm going to leave Cedarveil and go to a big city where nobody knows a single thing about me."

There's a pause while Pokey thinks. A blue heron glides over us, almost blending in against the flat-blue sky. I watch the heron disappear, wishing I could do the same.

Picture a Girl

"But I'd miss you," says Pokey. I know he is carefully not mentioning what Wendy said. He knows I don't want to talk about it. And that makes me love him more than ever.

The bell rings. We trudge back to the doors.

"I'd miss you too, Pokey," I admit. "But only you."

That makes him laugh. I wonder how I will tell Ms. Cranberg about the book. Whenever I talk to her in class or the library, I see that she wants to know what I have to say. What I want to read. Maybe she even has high expectations of me. I don't want that to ever change.

Pokey and I wait for Billy by the metal fence beside the jungle gym the Wisharts funded. Pokey stands quietly, not pushing me to talk. He is the best kind of friend that way. The stained library book is shoved in the bottom of my knapsack. I feel like it is glowing. I try to tell myself positive thoughts. Like, *I will think of something. I always do.* Mama is a big believer is positive thinking: "Believe in yourself, Adelaide. No one else can do that for you."

When she's not feeling so positive, she goes on one of these "adventures." Sometimes she travels all the way to Vancouver to see her friend Sara, hitchhiking to the ferry and then walking onto the boat. Sometimes she stays on Vancouver Island and heads to Campbell River or Victoria. The worst part is not knowing where she's gone or when she'll come back. It all started a couple of years ago, after she had to stop taking the pills for her back.

"Got any food?" Billy asks us, instead of saying hello. He can be downright rude, that one. Especially when he's tired and hungry.

"Got any food, *please*," I correct. "And no, I don't."

I have a blister on the bottom of my heel, and it feels like a warm, fat slug stuck there. I'm sick of walking all the time. Even if I were old enough to drive, we don't have a car anymore, because we can't afford the insurance or the gas.

"I have food," says Pokey, because he always does. Pokey is a big kid, a head taller even than me, and sturdy. He's one reason kids don't push me around more than they do. That plus I try to fly under the radar. Pokey pulls out a bag of white-cheddar kettle corn, and my mouth waters. "Help yourself," he says, handing the bag to Billy, who immediately crams a handful into his mouth, his lips dusted with the cheese.

We walk together in easy silence. Pokey and I don't need to talk all the time, not like Wendy and Layna, who are always gabbing, usually about other kids. I find endless talking exhausting, even though I am happy to have Pokey and Billy alongside me. I like to listen to the birds chattering to each other, or even to the sound of the cars sliding by. On rainy afternoons, back when we had the car, I used to hope sometimes that my mother would show up to drive me home. But she rarely did. We always walked. "Cars are bad for the environment anyway," she says.

"Did you have a good day?" I ask Billy. I used to ask him, "Did you behave in class?" but then I realized that was too negative. Billy can be restless. He has trouble sitting still. He gets frustrated with his reading.

"Yeah, I guess," he says, chewing on some popcorn. "But Ms. Chan wants to have a meeting with Mama."

I stop in my tracks. This is not good.

"Why?" I ask. "When?"

"I got a note," says Billy, not really answering the question.

"Let me see it."

He produces a scrap of paper. He has already managed to roll it up, like an ancient scroll.

Dear Ms. Scratch,

I am writing to request an in-person meeting with you on Friday, May 21, to discuss various issues with Billy concerning meeting expectations and classroom behavior. I was unable to reach you by phone or email…

Mama had a cell phone once, but we couldn't keep up with the bills. Mama insists she likes talking to people in person anyway. Now I've got a big problem. A teacher meeting and no Mama in sight.

"Is Mama going to be able to make it?" asks Billy.

I frown, not wanting to talk about it in front of Pokey. As far as he knows, Mama is coming home every night.

"Sure she will, you know that. She'll be home waiting for us," I say, though it's probably not true. Just saying the lie lodges something hard against my chest. It hurts that I can't even tell Pokey that Mama sometimes goes away. If someone found out, a grown-up, we'd be in big trouble. Despite how frustrating she is, I miss Mama badly. Her singing and the French toast she makes with cinnamon and vanilla. The way she tells me, "You can do anything you set your mind to, Adelaide."

Picture a Girl

I shove the note into my knapsack because I see Wendy Wishart's little sister, Evie, skipping toward us from the opposite side of the street. We spent so long waiting for Billy that the crossing guard, Walt, has gone home. Evie must have forgotten something in her classroom, maybe her lunch bag, because she's skipping along toward the school with empty hands and a smile on her face. Evie, unlike Wendy, is a breath of sunshine—always cheerful and friendly. More than once she's offered Billy half of her snack at recess when she's seen he doesn't have one. She doesn't make a big deal about it either. Evie loves show tunes, and she's humming a song from *Wicked,* the one about gravity, as she bounces along, her blond hair swinging. She's as sweet as Wendy is sour. It's hard to believe they came from the same place.

"Hey, Evie," I say. "Did you forget something?"

"Nope, Addie," she says, crinkling her freckled nose. "I mean, yup. My backpack. Mommy gets mad."

I understand that. I've heard Mrs. Wishart let loose on a few occasions.

"Okay, Evie, well, run on now. Is someone walking with you?"

"Nope," she says, giggling and skipping off. Evie is only in first grade, so she doesn't usually walk on her own, even in our small town. In the winter, Cedarveil only has about 2,000 people. In the summer every parking lot is full, and our grocery store runs out of potato chips and ice cream and camera batteries. Instagram has made it worse, especially since Cedarveil landed on a list of "Surf Towns You Gotta See." Sometimes campers even try to pitch their tents right by our cabin. Mama chases them off quickly enough. The May long weekend is around the corner, which means the start of the high season—or the silly season, as Mama calls it. She says we might as well fire a starting pistol at the end of May: Let the games begin. Pokey and Billy and I start walking again, and I wonder where Mama is this time. She can't even call us because we don't have a phone. *Please let her come back tonight so she can go to Billy's teacher meeting. Please.*

That word, *meeting*, is looming so large in my head, like those big block letters in the Hollywood sign you always see on TV shows, that I don't hear the car coming—but I see it. I can tell right away that it's a tourist car, someone from away getting an early start on the holiday weekend. The car is too big and too shiny to be from here. Almost everyone local has a pickup truck or a dented cube van. Vehicles here need to pull boats or haul surfboards or drive tourists around. The car is blue-black, sleek and silent like a shark as it speeds through the school zone. I hear Billy scream, and that makes my thoughts start churning red, like a siren. The driver, a woman in mirrored sunglasses, is turning her head, looking for a café or a visitor's center, oblivious to the fact that a six-year-old girl, Evie, is dancing across the intersection, skipping and singing.

I try to yell "Evie!" but my throat is as dry as plywood. I see the car's bumper closing in on her, and then Evie looks back and starts screaming too. I run off the sidewalk, toward the car…and then I'm down by the curb, lying on my side. Evie's not there anymore. My leg hurts but not too bad.

Pokey is yelling my name, "Addie, Addie," and a car door slams and grown-up voices are shouting. The noise has drawn a crowd from the school as well as from the nearby café, and there's a circle of people around me. Evie, I realize, is behind me on the sidewalk, where I pushed her out of the way. She begins to cry as if a stopper has been pulled. A stopper that was holding back Niagara Falls. Billy, in a startling moment of tenderness, has scampered to my side, burying his face in my shoulder.

I wiggle my face, then my legs and arms. I think I am okay.

"Can you move?" asks Billy.

I answer by sitting up, dizzy from the adrenaline but otherwise fine.

"Addie," says Pokey, standing to the side of me. "You saved her life."

"I'm so sorry," gasps the driver, a woman with frosted hair standing by her open car door. "I didn't see her."

Martin from the So Clean and Henriette from the café rush to me, helping me to my feet. I tell them I'm fine, I'm fine, so they turn their sights to Evie. She's still sniffling but talking. Her lip is trembling, but she seems okay. Martin and Henriette will make sure she gets home.

Now a whole crowd has gathered, making noise and taking pictures with their phones. There are too many adults here. I've got to go.

"Let's get out of here," I mutter.

I grab Billy's hand and start running before things get even more complicated.

I do only half of my math pages that night. I skip my push-ups and my jump-rope exercise. I'm too hungry to care. Billy and I split a can of tuna that I place on some salad greens I found in a tub at the back of the fridge. The tuna makes the whole cabin smell fishy.

"I wish I had a Captain's burger," moans Billy, looking down at his plate. The plate is sturdy and white, with little pink seashells around the rim. Mama found it at the Sally Ann, so we only have one. She loves to bring home little pieces of magic.

The Captain's burger is Billy's favorite. It includes an onion ring layered onto the patty, along with pickle, mayonnaise and a slice of back bacon. They serve it at Schooner's Café, where we go on special occasions, meaning almost never. When Grandma Lynn visited all the way from Australia, she took us there for burgers and strawberry milkshakes. Mama stayed home, saying she didn't like meat, but really, it was that she doesn't like our dad's mother. They've kept in touch, though. They are *civil*, as Mama puts it. There were a lot of moments during that dinner at Schooner's that you might call *awkward*, since it should have been our dad sitting across from us. I remember watching the ice cubes melt in Grandma Lynn's iced tea and wondering why he didn't want to see us. Grandma Lynn said it's because we live on an island. I guess anywhere can be an island if you aren't willing to make any effort. Even Australia is an island, just a really big one.

Our dad was Australian. He *is* Australian. He's not dead or anything, as far as we know. He works as an agronomist in rural Australia, or at least that's what Grandma Lynn told us. She has this strong, twangy accent that Billy likes to imitate. Agronomy has to do with soil and the science of growing things. Which makes him sound like a good guy. We asked Grandma Lynn so many questions, like where was Grandpa Cal, her husband (he has a heart condition, not good with long travel) and what was Australia like (wild in places, like Cedarveil; oceans, like here but with warm water; sandy beaches; and vicious jellylike creatures called bluebottles). Billy had asked what Australians eat.

"Lamb," answered Grandma Lynn, polishing her fork with a napkin. Nothing was ever clean enough for her, it seemed. She'd kept dabbing at Billy's face, as if wishing something away.

The last time she visited was a year ago, during Australia's autumn. Grandma Lynn stayed in a resort, the one owned by the Wisharts. I guess my dad's family has more money than us. At the end of the meal at Schooner's, she handed me an envelope to give to my mom and gave us each a stiff hug and a peck on the cheek.

"Grandma Lynn loves you," she said, as if speaking on someone else's behalf.

"Me too," I said, even though I wasn't sure. I was confused. Why did my dad never visit? Was agronomy that important?

Grandma Lynn also gave us extra cash to take a taxi home from the restaurant, which I kept in my shorts pocket. It would have been too weird to take a taxi to the end of our little road. Besides, you have to hike in to the cabin anyway. A taxi would have drawn the attention of Mr. Chadawack, who is already too nosy. But I didn't want to refuse the twenty dollars. We always needed money.

"Addie," asked Billy, after we had been walking in silence that night, listening to birds gossiping and the cars swooshing by with their radio songs streaking through the air.

"Yes?"

"Why doesn't our dad come to visit us?"

It was the one question we could never ask Grandma Lynn. The last time we saw our dad, Nick, was before we moved to Cedarveil. I barely remember him—and I don't think Billy recalls anything. We were still in Victoria, and Nick had stopped there for a day after attending a conference in Seattle. I remember playing Frisbee with him in a park downtown and him buying me soft-serve vanilla ice cream.

"It's just a long way," I had told Billy, picking up his hand to give it a squeeze. He still talks about that Captain's burger, though. He's not going to get one anytime soon.

"Addie," he asks, breaking into my memories. "Can you tell me a story tonight?"

I nod. "But only if you eat your dinner."

He grimaces but also nods. We can't afford to waste food. My stomach still growls as I squirt lemon soap in the sink. I never do a good job on the dishes, but it's better than nothing. As I wash, I think about Mama, and my thoughts bumper-car between being furious with her and hoping she is okay. She calls these trips "health breaks," even though sometimes they involve drinking with old friends in Vancouver and other times she just goes off hiking somewhere. I guess she gets tired of being our mom and worrying about money and the future and needs to get away. When she returns, she can be so fun, with her songs and special stories. She is the best when she is happy. It's like her love makes a magic chalk circle around you.

"What story do you want, Billy?" I ask, though I am already guessing what it will be.

Later, once our teeth are brushed, we lie on Mama's bed, me at one end and Billy at the other so we face each other, ready for me to begin.

WHEN MAMA MET NICK

"Picture a day so bright that the sun waters your eyes as you stare at a white-sand beach—it's called Bondi, in Sydney, Australia, a long way from here."

Mama's stories always start with you being asked to picture something. It's up to the listener to do their part.

"Bondi has an outdoor pool, right on the ocean, and sparkling blue water that shines like peacock feathers. Mama, age twenty-one, was spending a few days in Sydney as part of a trip that had already taken her to Thailand, Malaysia and Vietnam. She was running out of money, so she was sitting on a borrowed surfboard and eating a toastie, which is an Australian grilled cheese.

"Mama had forty dollars in Australian money and a plane ticket home, that's it. She had started the trip with two girlfriends, both of whom had already returned to Canada. She had to either find a way to make some money or go home with her prepaid plane ticket. But for that moment, she was staring at the waves crashing, listening to the birds calling and the children laughing, while eating that hot sandwich. Her hair was fashioned in two messy braids, or plaits, as they say in Australia, a look she still favors.

"She held the sandwich, intending to savor it. She wasn't sure what to do next with her life. There was nothing waiting for her at home—no job, no apartment. A seagull darted through the air, saw her vulnerability and dive-bombed toward her, soaring away toward the sun with the sandwich clamped in its beak.

"Mama, who was just called Jeanie Scratch then, watched the bird disappear. Her eyes filled with tears, because she was so, so hungry. Now she had nothing but a backpack full of dirty clothes and the beat-up surfboard she'd borrowed from someone at the hostel. Then, as the tears in her eyes cleared, she saw a young man standing in front of her. He wore red shorts and a yellow-and-red T-shirt. He was tall and lean, a street sign of a man, with long, ropey muscles and a swipe of white sunblock across his nose.

"'Everything all right, miss?' he asked her.

"'Yes,' she said, then changed her answer. 'No. That bird took my last meal.'

"Looking closer, she could see his shirt read *Lifeguard*. He was there working. For Bondi Beach is a dangerous place, with undertows and sharks and stinging creatures everywhere.

"'Bloody birds,' he muttered, trying not to grin.

"She introduced herself as Jeanie Scratch from Vancouver Island, Canada. He was Nick Wright from Greenwich, Sydney.

"'I'm off for the day. Can I buy you lunch?' he asked.

"She shook her head. Mama has always been independent. They struck a bargain. If she could catch the next wave, he would buy her lunch. If she failed…well, they didn't plan for that. He wanted to buy her lunch. And she wanted to spend more time with him. Mama, then just Jeanie, paddled out under the fiery sun and caught a monster wave. She carved and turned like a ball in a pinball machine.

When she scrambled up on the beach, gasping and dripping water on the sand, her heart was pounding, her face shining.

"Nick, our dad, grinned.

"'Now you got to try that in icy-cold water, which is what it's like where I'm from,' she told him, planting the borrowed board back in the sand.

"'Us Aussies don't do cold,' he said, shaking his head and backing away playfully.

"Jeanie laughed.

"He had made her smile. And he had won her heart."

Billy always says that last line along with her. The rest of the story gets somewhat messy, and Mama usually doesn't go into it much. We know they fell in love and lived in Sydney, and then eventually he had to go back to university. She couldn't find work and didn't have the proper documents. They stayed together anyway. They fought. And somewhere during all that, Adelaide Elizabeth Scratch was born. I was named Adelaide after the Australian city, and Elizabeth after my mom's grandmother, who died when I was three.

"That's the end of the story," I say, to make it clear I'm not getting into all that.

Billy sighs, his chin tucked into his chest like he's going to do a dive off a high board. "Can I sleep next to you tonight?" he asks.

I nod, because I know he is feeling like his skin is exposed and raw. I feel the same when she's away. We are both already lying on my mother's quilt, so it is easy to stay there. I wedge a line of pillows in the space between us, because Billy thrashes around when he sleeps, and I don't want him to sock me in the face.

WEDNESDAY

I wake up smelling burnt coffee. Even though I'm half-awake, my heart does a little flutter as I wonder if Mama came home in the night, crept into her bed and has now made coffee, hoping to start the day off right. Then I realize the smell is just from my dream. We are lying in Mama's bed, still covered in the yellow-and-green patchwork quilt she inherited from her mother, Grandma Lillian, who inherited it from her mother, Elizabeth. I feel the soft dent in the middle where the mattress sags slightly from bearing Mama's weight—thin as she is—night after night.

I get out of bed and smooth the quilt, feeling the bump of the hand stitching. The clack of the second hand over the stove tells me it's past time to get Billy up. As I look at his slack sleeping face, I feel a current of anger run through me. I love Billy, and he's a part of me—like my two hands—but I don't want to look after him all the time. I shake his shoulder gently, forcing myself not to be rough.

Why can't he wake himself up? He's eight, after all. When I was eight, I had to grow up. Before that things were better. Grandma Lillian and her new husband, Grandpa Earl, would come and check on Mama. We lived in an apartment in Victoria then, I remember, a small city by the sea without much of a surf scene. Grandpa Earl was a calm, big-chested man who always wore plaid golf shirts and ball caps, and he helped keep Grandma Lillian and Mama from bickering over the past. But he died soon after I turned eight.

"Do you remember when we lived in Victoria?" I ask Billy, even though he's just waking up and probably doesn't know what planet he's on.

"What?" he asks, rubbing his eyes. "Was that the place with the pool?"

I think for a second and realize he's right. We had a first-floor apartment in a big building downtown called Holiday House. Our apartment had a concrete pool in the basement of the building, and Mama worked as a prep cook in a cafeteria. It was one of Mama's better jobs, but she got agitated from not surfing. We loaded up our brown-paneled station wagon and left in the middle of the night so we could skip out on our lease. I was seven, and Billy was four.

We were happy there, from what I remember. Our apartment smelled like the day-old cinnamon buns Mama would bring home.

My stomach rumbles now as I open the cupboards to scrounge for food. I shift the bag of wheat flour to locate the packets of instant oatmeal—maple, the best kind. I put the kettle on.

"Let's eat fast. Pokey will be waiting for us," I say.

Billy likes Pokey, luckily. Billy loves soccer, and Pokey is super good at it, so Billy admires him. Pokey becomes a different person on the soccer field, fast and fearless.

We gulp down the sweet, powdery oatmeal, so much less filling than the hearty steel-cut oats and berries Mama sometimes stirs up on the stove (much better than when I make it). *When she was good, she was very, very good.* That's my mother, in a way, just like the girl in the nursery rhyme, with a curl right in the middle of her forehead. I lock the cabin, do a quick scan for bears or cougars—because you never know—and sling on my knapsack.

"Where do you two think you're going?" I hear, and I jump like a snake just fell on my head.

It's our landlord, Mr. Chadawack, who isn't usually around this early. He stays up late in the lobby of the resort, listening to the radio and gambling online. Mama says he sometimes loses a lot of money, which makes him mad at the world. When I see him, I start hoping he had a winning streak last night.

"I'm just kidding. I know you're going to school," he says, smiling. His face is red all year round. He has small spider veins in his nose, like little rivers. I ball my fist up like I do when I'm scared. He usually only visits our cabin when he wants something. And I can't let him know Mama isn't here.

"Yes," I say, trying to sound sure and confident. "Got a big math test today." I add that detail because I know it makes it even more believable, even though it's the truth. I've heard Mama tell her share of tall tales. I've learned how to talk my way out of a situation.

"Your mom at home? I need to talk to her," he says, staring hard, as if daring us to fib.

"No. She left early to work a shift at the Bent Bow," I say, scraping out a lie that could be true. Mama sometimes picks up cleaning shifts at the Bent Bow Motel. Still, I don't like lying, even to Chadawack. Sometimes I don't tell Billy the whole truth, but that's different. That's to save his feelings.

"Let's go, Billy," I add. "We're going to be late."

It was a long, rainy day at school. Billy, for once, was cooperative and quiet when we got home in the afternoon. He even tried to do his home reading, as best he could. I kept watching the door, worried Chadawack would return. Now, after heating up some beans for dinner, I am done. I have nothing more.

"It's too late for a story tonight," I tell him.

"Please," he whines.

"No," I say firmly. He must be exhausted, because he crawls under the covers, still wearing his clothes. I lie on Mama's bed, on Elizabeth's quilt, thinking. There is the story of Lillian, our grandmother, and how she never hugged my mom, often leaving her alone at night in their townhouse in Comox. How she made Jeanie vacuum the whole house and wash sheets and cook meals for the boarders who lived with them when she was only seven years old—because "hard work never hurt anyone." How Jeanie ran away when she was a teenager, first to Vancouver, then to southern California, where she discovered surfing—then to the very tip of Vancouver Island, where she discovered cold-water surfing, the kind where you bring a thermos of hot water to pour over your numb fingers afterward.

Lillian's own mother, my great-grandmother Elizabeth, came to Canada during the war, as something called a "home child." It meant leaving all her own relatives in England to work on a farm in the Cowichan Valley.

"They treated her like a maid," Mama said. "They never hugged her or gave her enough to eat. She never knew what mothers were supposed to do. Lillian never learned either."

Mama always ended the story that way, mentioning Lillian. Mama said she didn't believe in talking down to kids, so she told us the truth, at least as she understood it. I switch off my mother's reading lamp, close my eyes and tell myself a story.

ELIZABETH'S STORY

Picture a girl. She has a long, sloping nose, brown eyes and a sad, downturned mouth. Her hair is brushed neatly, and someone has tacked a floppy white bow to one side of her head. That's the one photo I've seen of her, my great-grandmother Elizabeth. She was born small, red and wailing in 1938 to parents Jean and Kenneth, joining two brothers and two sisters. The family lived above a butcher shop in a two-room flat in London, England. Kenneth worked shifts at a nail factory. Elizabeth, called Betty, slept in a single bed with her sisters, Olive and Hazel. The boys, Kenneth Jr. and Brian, slept in another.

Then one day, Kenneth, their dad, was found unconscious in the storeroom of the factory. He died two days later in a hospital bed. Jean had almost no savings, a sixth-grade education and five children to feed. When the money ran out, Jean was left with the choice of watching her children starve or sending them away. She decided to send the three youngest to Canada in the hopes they would have better lives. The selling points were fresh air, healthy food and clean living on the farm. Elizabeth and her sister, Hazel, traveled by ship with dozens of other British children and wound up at a farm in the Cowichan Valley. There, they worked in the kitchen, soaked their pillows with tears every night and spoke as little as possible.

Their brother, Brian, was shipped somewhere else in the country, and they never saw him again. By the time they traced his path years later to rural Quebec, it was too late. Brian had died of pancreatic cancer at the age of fifty-eight.

The sisters survived on the farm, talking to no one but each other, often walking with their arms linked, as if one of them were sighted and the other were blind. They never understood why their mother had let them go. They would stay up late telling each other stories of home—the foods, the sounds of London, the family lore—to keep their past alive, even as a faint ember. The stories were all they had left. There were letters that dripped in from London, but they eventually stopped without explanation, like a spigot turned off.

Hazel married a farm-machinery repairman and moved to the Prairies. So the sisters were split up, and Elizabeth was spat out into the world alone, like a bitter seed into the wind. Elizabeth married a cruel man who owned a hardware store in Comox on Vancouver Island. She had her own daughter, Lillian—our mom's mom. Elizabeth had forgotten what it was like to give tenderness or receive it, and she rarely hugged Lillian or offered her praise.

When Lillian won a gold medal at a school track meet, her mother asked, "What good is that?" By then Elizabeth had forgotten how, back in England, her mother, Jean, used to brush her hair for her and pin it back with bobby pins. She had forgotten the way Jean had rubbed Elizabeth's back in circles when she couldn't sleep, or the way her older brother Kenneth Jr. had told jokes. She'd mostly forgotten about her lost older sister, Olive, or that anyone had ever called her Betty.

Mama only told me this story once, so I keep the details close. Sometimes I wonder if that sadness was handed down from Elizabeth to Lillian and on to Mama. I like to imagine the sisters holding hands on the farm. Or maybe Hazel rubbed Betty's back when she couldn't sleep, like her mom once had. Perhaps they helped pick crisp farm apples, the sweet white flesh shot through with delicate red veins. I hope they ate the apples. I hope there was at least some sweetness in their young lives.

My cottony thoughts of Elizabeth and Lillian are interrupted by Billy's whisper, which always seems loud in the thick darkness of our little cabin.

"Addie," he hisses, standing by my bed and tapping me on the forearm with one finger. I hate when he does that, the tapping. It feels like a bird pecking my arm.

"What, Billy? You should be asleep."

"I know," he says. "But I'm worried."

"About what?" I say, even though I know.

"Mama," he says, sighing. "I wonder where she is."

"Get to sleep. You've got school tomorrow," I say, just like Mama would. She always wanted us to be rested for school. We could sleep in on Saturdays, but we hardly ever did, not if the surf was good. The best weekends were when we all hit the beach together in our wetsuits. Billy wasn't that strong a surfer yet, but Mama was giving him tips. After I had tried to ride a couple of waves, I would sit on the shore, hugging my legs, watching her go. It was like watching King James score a three-pointer or Mozart conduct a symphony or whatever. We were all happiest in the water, we three Scratches. I never felt poor or strange paddling in the surf. I knew why she loved it, because I did too. It made me felt settled and alive at the same time.

Those were the very best days. We'd hike back to the cabin and peel out of our wetsuits before devouring scrambled eggs or French toast and hot cocoa, if we had the provisions. I was always so hungry after being in the cold.

I have a secret that I keep from Billy. Sometimes I feel as if it's an anchor that I drag along behind me. Here it is: Nick can't really be his dad. I figured it out last year, when I was looking through Mama's drawer of old photographs. She often scrawled the place and date on the back.

Mama moved away from Australia a year and a half before Billy was born. I know how long it takes to make a baby. And Nick Wright only visited Canada once, for the Seattle conference—long after Billy was born. Grandma Lynn always says he'll make the trip someday, but he never does. It's okay. Sometimes I wish I had a dad, if I had a nice one like Pokey does. Other times, I try to be happy with what I have.

THURSDAY

I have the beach to myself in the morning, the sky streaked gray wool. I'm shaking at first, tired and hungry, but I get a little better every time I catch a wave. Saturday is coming fast. But for now, I have to hurry back to the cabin, my board at my side, or we'll be late for school. Later in the day, I ace a math test, which gives me a little jolt of hope. But once we're home again, the cabin seems gloomy. The kitchen floor needs cleaning, and the fridge smells.

Billy has had enough. He's reached his limit of patience with Mama being gone. He misses her. He misses her bedtime stories. Plus, he gripes about how we have no Wi-Fi and no Xbox. He wants to do the same things other kids do after school—eat ketchup chips and play games.

"It's not *faaaair*," he says.

"Ms. Chan is concerned about your reading," I say to him, trying to change the subject. "Want to take some books to the beach?" Billy almost always calms down on the beach. It was his daycare when he was tiny, and now it's his backyard.

"No," he snaps. "I hate reading."

"Reading is stories," I tell him. "Just like in the cabin."

"It's not the same," he pouts, sticking out his bow-shaped lip. He kicks at the leg of our kitchen table, knocking off a chip of the green paint. I resist yelling at him, again, for kicking the table.

"Come on. Maybe we'll find some bottles to return. Or some glass floats."

He nods, so I give us each a few sprays of sunscreen. (Mama says Scratches are known to burn, so we can't skip it.) He has a swipe of dirt across his face and needs a good, soapy shower, but that can wait. I throw his book and few other things into a fabric drawstring bag and lock the cabin behind us.

The floats are old glass balls that fishermen used to attach to their nets. Tourists collect them, and they can bring in quite a few dollars at the antique store. I can tell there's not enough wind to surf, but I want to get out of the cabin and put some space between us. Plus, if we scrounge up some change, we can get popsicles from the store at the campground.

I feel better as soon as we step out into the forest, smell the warmed cedar, feel the pine needles gently prick my heels through my sandals. Two minutes later we are out on the bright, open space of Aerie Beach. It still startles me to walk from the trees onto the sunlit beach—it's like having a green velvet curtain thrown open. A few tourists are dotted along the sand—just a warm-up for the tsunami of visitors ahead in the summer months. I scan the shore, noting that someone has dismantled the driftwood fort we made last week.

A gray-haired couple in matching yellow gumboots is taking photos and beachcombing. They even wear identical sun hats—the kind that look like canvas boats. A family of four—a mom, a dad, a boy and a girl—has scattered gear everywhere: a play tent, umbrella, kid-sized volleyball net and even a bright-yellow battery-operated toy car. I see Billy notice the car. He's always wanted one like that, though Mama claims they are hunks of junk. The family has plastic shopping bags of groceries they've brought to the beach, which would make Mama go *off*. She goes bananas if she finds a plastic bag in the water. A science book I read showed a pile of plastic bags that biologists had removed from one whale's stomach. The photo made me angry and sad at the same time.

The cool ocean breeze kisses my face, and I close my eyes for a second to breathe in the salty smell. When I open them, I see the two kids staring right at me. Billy, in turn, can't take his eyes off the battery-operated car. The boy, who is about Billy's size, notices this and turns all his attention to it. The boy climbs in, sits on the driver's seat and presses a button. It doesn't roll far in the wet sand, so he gets out again, glares at Billy. I can tell we're not going to get any reading done. The beach is too busy. I grab a ball from my bag, ignoring the book I brought for Billy.

"I brought a football," I say to him. "Let's play."

Billy nods and backs up toward the small parking lot that is often jammed with minivans and cars with out-of-province license plates. I throw a pass to him, gripping it the way my mother taught me. Just before the release, I flick my wrist to make a spiral. Billy catches it and raises his eyebrows, impressed.

"Admit it," I say, smiling. "That was a perfect throw."

He lobs it back, imitating my snap. His spiral is pretty good.

"Where do you think she is today?" he asks, as we throw and catch. I run for one that ends up landing in the sand. Moving makes me feel better. Helps me tamp down my anxiety about the contest.

"Dunno," I say. "Maybe Victoria? Or Vancouver. I'm sure she'll be back soon."

I know she gets sad. Sometimes she needs to be by herself. Once she went to a music festival on one of the Gulf Islands and brought us back handmade wooden recorders. She never gives us a real reason for her departures, and I never ask. It's part of our bargain. I guess I'm afraid that she'll say she leaves because of me, that she needs space from *me*.

My next throw is too hard, and it sails past Billy into the parking area, bouncing off the window of a big gray minivan. The football ricochets toward the family, thumping down next to a Starbucks cup they've brought from the next town over, because there isn't one in Cedarveil. The best coffee in town is at Henriette's Coffee, where she serves two different kinds of dark roast and raspberry scones the size of softballs. That's where I tell the tourists to go if they seem nice. Maybe I would have told the gumboot couple about it, but they seem to have left.

"Hey, don't be hitting my Levante," says the dad, giving us a forced smile. At first I think Levante might be the boy's name, then realize, like a dummy, that it's the make of his car.

"I won't," I say, and I throw the ball back to Billy. I don't want to go back to the empty cabin yet, but I feel the family watching us. The mom is lounging on a striped towel, a big straw sun hat fastened under her chin. She has a little foam separator to keep her toes apart and is painting her toenails while sitting on the beach, her lips pursed as if it's a super-urgent task.

Billy catches the ball, and I take a deep breath of the sea air. The cabin currently smells like bananas and feet. There's nothing good for dinner, and my stomach feels as if someone is dragging it along a cheese grater. Nerves. The surf contest. Sometimes I wonder why I want to win so badly. I'm not even sure. I guess I want to show everyone not to count me out.

Billy pulls his arm back and lobs the ball, also too hard, so that it flies toward the shore where the other boy sits behind the wheel of his yellow car, looking bored. The football thumps down next to the boy, sending a spray of wet sand onto the plastic seat. At the same time, a gust of wind sends a plastic shopping bag ballooning away from the family's picnic spread, skidding to the shoreline.

"You should be more careful!" the dad yells, spit flying from his mouth.

He has round, gold-rimmed glasses and a spiky, carefully gelled hairstyle. They probably thought they'd beat the crowd for the May long weekend. They didn't count on having two local kids on the beach, spraying sand and ruining their Instagram photos. I take in the dad and his expensive everything, and the stupid foam thing that his wife uses to hold her toes in place, and it makes me so mad that I curl my fingers into a fist.

"Why don't *you* be more careful?" I say to him, my voice surprising me. It's clear and loud. "That's *your* plastic bag." I point to where it is sagging in the water, looking like a sick jellyfish. "Did you know that shorebirds and whales consume them, thinking they're food?"

I start to shake slightly, like the dishes did the time we had the magnitude 4.5 earthquake. The dad stares at me, apparently shocked that I talked back to him. Adelaide Elizabeth Scratch is not usually one to talk back. She gets along with others—or at least that's what her report cards say.

"Did you know," I say, "that the plastic makes whales think they're full, so they stop eating?"

He stares at me blankly. The mom adjusts her big sun hat to get a better look at me. She's wearing a long navy dress, the kind that ties in front. Suddenly I am more interesting to her than her toenails.

"I…" He thinks for a second. "I think I did know that."

"Did you know that scientists in Japan accidentally created a mutant enzyme that eats plastic? But we still need to recycle."

"Dylan, can you fetch that plastic bag, please?"

Dylan, the boy, scowls, first at me, then at his dad, then at Billy, even though Billy had nothing to do with it. Dylan saunters to the shore and pulls out the soaked bag. The mother claps her hands as if her son had to punch a great white whale in the nose and grab the bag from its jaws.

"Thanks," I whisper, because I can't think of anything else to say. Goosebumps run up my arms, because it is getting too cold for my grimy red tank top. It used to be my favorite, but now the straps are frayed.

I walk over to the yellow car. I see that it's the exact kind Billy had wanted, except he pined for a red one. I grab the football, tuck it under my arm. I used to carry Billy around the same way, like a football, when he was a baby. Grandma Lillian taught me how.

Billy doesn't need to be told that it's time to leave. I want to let these people know that this is our backyard. That we're here in the winter, when the storms are tossing clumps of kelp on the beach and the rain is pelting down sideways like plump thumbtacks. We're here when the main road out of town gets blocked by a rockslide or a snowstorm. We're here when the wind knocks the power out and it takes three days to come back on. We're here when the earth rumbles and the shelves shake.

I say nothing, just pick up my drawstring bag and drop the football in. I hold Billy's hand on the way home, something we hardly ever do anymore. I hear an eagle's jangly call from somewhere in the trees.

"How did you learn all that about whales?" Billy asks as we cross the beach.

"I read about it in a book."

I see him considering that. He nods.

"Reading is food for your brain, Billy." It's something Ms. Cranberg says.

"My brain likes Captain's burgers with yam fries," says Billy, giving my hand a squeeze.

We are just about to start down the forest path when Billy turns around. The family has packed up and is loading all their gear into the Levante, or whatever it was called. The dad hoists the toy car up, brushing sand from its wheels. The boy, Dylan, has started yelling about something.

"It's like they lost interest in the beach the second we left," Billy says.

I had been thinking the exact same thing. Billy bugs me so much sometimes, but we can't help but be the same. Stubborn, observant, a bit petty.

"Now that they're gone, I kind of want to go back," I say.

He grins again. He hasn't been smiling much.

"Oh. Em. Gee," says Billy suddenly.

"What?"

He drops my hand and runs to the spot in the sand where the yellow toy car was sitting. He yells, sweeping his hand behind a large, jagged rock, right next to the dip in the sand where the car had been. He pulls out a Japanese float and holds it up in the air.

"Hey," I shout, running to him. A float sells for as much as thirty dollars at the Antiques and Curiosities shop. Tourists love them—and we can get ten dollars for bringing one in. Billy holds the float up for me to admire. It's a sea-green beauty covered in a black web of netting. I let my eyes get lost in its maze of light and color. It's like gazing into an underground cave where mysterious things might dart out.

"This is a good one," I tell Billy. "I bet you can get more than ten dollars for that." It's the size of a bowling ball and looks as if it's been in the water for a long time.

"We'll take it into the antique shop tomorrow," he says.

I can tell he's already dreaming about what he can buy—a pack of Skittles, an Avengers comic. We should use the money to buy groceries—eggs and peanut butter and macaroni—but he hasn't had any good surprises in a while. I remember looking up the glass floats on eBay, using the library internet. They'd go for $45 US sometimes, if they were really special. *Ocean survivor*, one listing said. I wondered what had happened to the person who owned the boat, whether they'd made it home to Japan.

We head home quickly since it's getting late. I open the cabin door to find that dark has already flooded the cabin. It reminds me of the way Peter Pan's shadow creeps around after him in that old Disney movie, one of the ones we watched at

Pokey's house. Pokey has no brothers or sisters, so he doesn't mind if Billy sometimes tags along to watch movies too.

I dash into the cabin, banging my hip on the kitchen chair no one pushed in. I start to turn on the lamps. When I do, my eyes adjust to see a large shadow sitting in my mother's pink velveteen armchair. It's a man, crouching there, waiting. I ball up my fists, a scream caught in my throat, and then everything comes into focus.

"Hi, Mr. Chadawack. I didn't know you were coming," I say through gritted teeth. Mama told me that by law, Chadawacky has to give us notice if he's entering our cabin. He can't just open the door and let himself in. He'd never do that to his summer people, the city people. I set my jaw and hear my teeth grind. The sound reminds me of barnacles crunching under my shoes.

"Your mother owes me the last half of May's rent. Now we're almost to June. She's getting behind on her payments."

I unclench my fist and try to smile. I've never liked Mr. Chadawack, even though he thinks I do. He's nice to us when it suits him. Other times he's moody and acts as if he's doing us a big favor by renting us the cabin. I want to tell him that the cabin is musty, the kitchen linoleum is cracked and the fridge door sticks. He likes to think the cabin is rustic luxury, and maybe it was ten or twenty years ago. Now the Storybook Cabin is faded and rundown. He upgrades the other cabins, the ones he rents to tourists, but always leaves ours for another day. Mr. Chadawack is cheap. I feel a surge of anger, like a stove element glowing on.

She should be here. She should be here to talk to Chadawack.

"My mom's working at Schooner's, helping prep the Captain's burgers," says Billy.

I try not to widen my eyes. I follow Mr. Chadawack's gaze. He's staring at the Japanese float sitting on the kitchen table.

"What's that?" asks Chadawack, his squinty eyes fixed on the float, its color glowing even in the dim light of the cabin. Finding that float is the only thing that's making Billy hold it together right now.

"Billy brought that home from school to study how it works," I say too loudly. "He has to bring it back to his teacher when his project is done."

Chadawack is smart enough to know that the float is worth some money and stupid enough to believe the lie. He could rent out our cabin for the summer in a heartbeat. Winter is another story.

That's why he hasn't kicked us out. Yet. But I suspect he's always thinking about it.

Chadawack just nods, then shakes his finger at us before turning toward the door. Maybe this gesture is for things we've done wrong that he doesn't know about—or things we might do in the future. He drinks a lot of beer and leaves the cans by the side of his house in a plastic bin. Sometimes Billy and I steal some of them to return at the bottle depot when we really need some change.

I lock the latch behind him. I cook some rice and heat up a can of black beans, then serve them together along with two mugs of apple-cinnamon herbal tea. It stops my stomach from growling but doesn't fill me up. Sometimes I think I'll never be full.

Billy slips into bed without asking for a story—or brushing his teeth. He also doesn't offer to help with the dishes. I decide to leave them.

I lie in my mother's bed that night, trying to smell her, to feel her presence. I fantasize about food, dreaming of fluffy pancakes stacked up high, soaked with butter and maple syrup. There's a security light outside that casts a thin, yellow light. I listen to the wind whistle through the trees outside, then rise up in the near dark to shove Mama's dresser against the cabin door, shunting it forward with my hip. Then, out of anger, I kick the old stereo that she uses to play her vintage vinyl records—Neil Young, David Bowie, Stevie Wonder, Joni Mitchell.

I don't want Chadawack to return. There is something slightly rotten about Chadawack, and I hate having him around when my mother is gone—or at any time.

A few minutes go by and I hear Billy sigh and start to gently snore. If my mother turns up tomorrow, I sure hope she brings food.

THE OTHER STORY I CAN NEVER TELL BILLY

Sometimes my mother forgets the endings to her own stories, especially if she's at the bottom of one of her brown bottles. I remember the endings for her. But not every story is hers. Some stories are mine. I carry that fact in my pocket like a cold, smooth stone that I sometimes touch to make sure it's still there.

One of the stories I can never tell happened when Billy was five years old.

We had just moved to Cedarveil from Victoria. The price was right for the cabin, and it was just a few paces from Aerie, a surfing beach. The cabin came sparsely furnished, and we'd unpacked our clothes and placed them in the heavy wooden dressers. Mama woke up at first light, wanting to go surfing. It was a gray, stormy late-August morning, and I didn't want to go to the beach. I howled, even though I was a big girl, eight years old. It would be cold and windy at the beach, but I didn't want to be left with Billy in the cabin either. It smelled funny to me, like pine cleaner and mold.

I was used to the apartment building in Victoria, with people above and below us and the ping of an elevator. I hadn't met Pokey yet and didn't know anyone in Cedarveil. The cabin had creaky floorboards and wet branches that whipped against the windows and lights that flickered when the wind howled. I was afraid, but Billy was snoring away in his little bed. I watched the rise and fall of his chest, annoyed that he could sleep so peacefully in this funny home.

"I'll just be a few minutes, Adelaide," Mama said. "The waves are gonna be perfect."

She grabbed the old T-shirt she used to wipe down her board and her square of wax. I usually liked to watch her wax her board, the way she'd stroke crosshatches on it to get a better grip on her feet. But that day I didn't want her to go. And I didn't want to look after Billy. I was nervous about starting a new school the next week. I wasn't in the mood.

"Take us with you," I said to Mama, grabbing her arm.

She was already wearing her black wetsuit. I didn't know how she'd paid for it. They cost a fair chunk of money. But she lived to surf. It was that simple. She'd found a way. Sometimes it infuriated me to remember how capable she could be.

"I don't want to wake up Billy," she said. "Back soon, Addie, and then we'll have French toast with cinnamon, 'kay? Look after Billy like a big girl."

I remember the sound of the door shutting—the frame is a bit warped, so you have to give it a good shove. I stood there, watching little Billy sleep, still unaware our mother had left us to go put herself in the middle of a storm. I could pretend that I locked the door after Mama and straightened the blanket over Billy and waited for her to come back—but I didn't. I zipped up a fleece jacket over my pajamas, yanked on my rubber Spider-Man boots and marched out after her, leaving Billy sleeping. I ran down the trail to the shore, the wind whipping my hair in my face, my fists balled up at my sides. I spotted her out alone in the pewter sea, watching the sets of waves, waiting. I held up my hand to her, but she didn't see me. I shouted to her, but she didn't hear me. I realized it didn't matter what I said or did or how I felt—she would surf until she was done.

I walked back to the cabin, stomping on the shells and rocks, crying and feeling sorry for myself, no one in sight to ask me what was wrong. When I got to the cabin, the door was wide open and Billy was gone. I felt my stomach flop to my feet. I ran inside still wearing my muddy boots and patted the dent on the bed where his little body had been. The blue flannel sheet was still warm. I tripped over one of the moving boxes and then checked the bathroom, shouting, "Billy! Billy!" If I didn't find him, Mama would be furious. And if somebody else found him, we'd all be in trouble. I ran back out into the woods, crashing through the brush and calling his name.

I was supposed to be a big girl, but I was only eight, just a little older than Evie. I was thinking the whole time, What will I do if Billy is gone? He was my little brother. My *only* brother. What if he was…gone? I pressed my hand to my chest, as if that would slow my racing heart. I called his name again, but it came out in a sob.

Then I found him, sitting under big Crooked Red, hugging his knees to himself. My knees nearly buckled under me with relief. He was still wearing his gray-striped pajamas, which were wet and plastered to his body.

"Hey, Billy," I said, now strangely calm as I stood under Crooked Red. The path leading to Crooked Red was rough back then, tangled with tree roots and deadfall. This was before the men came with the truck to make the path to the hot tub.

"You lost me," he said, staring up at me. Not looking angry, just confused.

"No," I said. "I *found* you." Which was kind of a lie, or at least a half-truth.

I managed to pick him up and carry him back home, his wet body seeming to weigh three times more than usual. His feet were like two popsicles, so I ran him a hot shower and found a fresh pair of pajamas for him. By the time Mama returned, vibrating with post-surf energy, he was sitting on the floor crashing Hot Wheels cars into each other.

That's how the story ends. I never told Mama about it, and Billy didn't tell her either. He's never mentioned that day, and I won't remind him.

I never want him to remember that I left him once too.

FRIDAY

I wake up itchy and hot because I've rolled myself up like a burrito in Elizabeth's quilt. This is our fifth day alone, almost a new record. The longest so far is eight days. I wonder if this is the time I should finally tell someone, Ms. Cranberg or Pokey or his mom. But then they might take us both away to a different home or, worse, separate us. I can't take that risk. I could also call Grandma Lillian, a thought that keeps bumping against the screen of my mind. But Mama would be angry. And Grandma Lillian would be angry at Mama—and at me for not calling earlier. I shove aside the idea for now.

The cabin is airless and stuffy. Sometimes when I open a window before bed, the slap of branches and the roar of the surf keeps me awake, worried and wondering. There's a knock at the cabin door, which nearly causes me to jump out of my skin, as if I were a snake that could leave my dried-out self behind. Mr. Chadawack again, I think. I push the dresser out of the way so I can peek out the small window in the door. I am so relieved that I bark a laugh when I see Pokey's face out there, peering in, waiting for me to open the door. Sometimes, if he's running early, he will walk all the way to our cabin.

"I come bearing eggs," says Pokey. "From Shakira and Beyoncé."

Pokey's mom, Mrs. Polk, inherited some chickens from a neighbor who sold their place to buy a condo in the city. The chickens came with names. Pokey really likes them, but he hates having to clean up the chicken coop. Sometimes I call them Shake and Bey just to bug him.

"Hey, thanks, Pokey," I say, sweeping my eyes around the cabin. I have just left my mother's bed, so he can't tell she didn't sleep in it. My own bed is still unmade too, mostly because I don't tidy it unless someone makes me.

Picture a Girl

Pokey doesn't ask where my mom is, and I say nothing, just run my fingers through my hair and take the cast-iron skillet off the hook on the wall. I yank open the fridge door and peer in. There's a square of butter wrapped in a piece of foil and a few inches of milk in a plastic carton. Scrambled eggs might just get Billy out of bed. My mouth fills with saliva as the butter hits the pan and sizzles. I use a fork to stir up the eggs with a splash of milk and then add a sprinkle of salt. Mama is a competent cook and showed me the basics. I learned by watching her.

"Can you keep an eye on these?" I ask Pokey, handing him the plastic spatula, warped on one side where I once left it against the burner and it melted, just like the bad guy's face in *Raiders of the Lost Ark*.

"Will do," says Pokey, who is almost always cheerful. Wendy Wishart and her friends used to try to make fun of Pokey, like how he speaks slowly even though he runs fast, or how he wears *Star Wars* T-shirts every day, always with striped Adidas pants or soccer shorts. No variation. On Wednesdays he wears Wookiees. On Mondays the T-shirt usually has Darth Vader. He's rocking a red one with an AT-AT walker today. His style is simple and, admittedly, a little strange. But Wendy and her friends couldn't get to him, so they gave up.

While he tends the eggs, I dash into our closet-sized bathroom and brush my hair, then run a washcloth over my face. I have a sprinkling of freckles on my nose, since we've seen a bit of May sunshine between the rains. I stare into my brown eyes and wonder if I look eleven. I feel older. I notice that a blue slug of toothpaste is clinging to the sink. It's time to get Billy up. Then I remember what day it is.

I throw the bathroom door open and call him. He'll need to look clean and presentable and mothered. Today's the meeting with Ms. Chan.

By the time we get to school, my stomach is cramping with anxiety, and I wish I hadn't eaten the plate of eggs, however good they tasted at the time. I've considered all kinds of tactics, including pulling the fire alarm at 2:50 p.m., just before the school day ends, so Ms. Chan will forget about the meeting. I was also thinking of signing a note asking for it to be postponed. I've got Mama's signature down pat. But I like Ms. Chan. I don't want to lie to her. She was my teacher in third grade, just after we moved here, and she always makes awesome lanterns for Chinese New Year.

When my mother didn't send a treat to share with the class on my birthday, Ms. Chan went to the Save Easy on her lunch break and bought mini vanilla cupcakes with sprinkles on top—and the class never knew they came from her. I reminded my mother every birthday after that.

"Pokey, I'll see you in class," I mumble, not looking at him. "I gotta do something."

I take Billy by the hand and tow him to his classroom, my ratty sneakers squeaking on the floors. For the first time in my life, I see clearly, as if someone twisted the focus on the binoculars raised to my eyes. I think I've been hiding it, but my teachers *know* my mom is different. They know. And all the extra things they do for me are because of that. I haven't fooled anyone. My eyes sting with tears, and I grip Billy's fingers harder.

"Ow," he says, pulling his hand away.

I snatch it back, angry. At him. At Mama. At everyone. If I am not angry, I will cry, and I can't cry. Adelaide Elizabeth Scratch will not cry in front of people. I knock on Ms. Chan's door, which is wedged partly open. A hand-painted sign on it says *Welcome* in about ten different languages, and there are little cartoons on it—a rabbit, a wolf, an elephant, a tiger, all of them smiling. The elephant is wearing a gray flat-top cap like he's a bus driver.

"Come in," says Ms. Chan.

She is seated at her desk, reviewing her plan for the day. She has a mug of coffee with cream beside her, just like she used to when she was my teacher.

"Oh, hi, Adelaide, Billy. How can I help you?"

She waits, smiling. She's wearing a cobalt-blue V-neck blouse with a pewter starfish pendant that I recognize from when she taught me.

"It's about the meeting today," I begin.

Ms. Chan nods and takes a sip of the coffee. "I'm looking forward to seeing your mother again."

"Well, the thing, is," I say. "You know, we don't really have a phone right now. My mom says they kill your attention span."

We don't have a phone at all, is the truth. No smartphone, no cell phone, not even an emergency satellite phone. Nothing. Saying it out loud is embarrassing. Most kids have their phones at their sides all the time, like Jedis with their lightsabers. When we really need to call somebody, we have to go to Mr. Chadawack's office—and listen to his complaints. Mama had a cell plan until January, when the jobs thinned out in the off-season. Then she couldn't pay the bill and the service got cut off. No phone is better, in a way, because then she can't call people when she is angry or has drunk too much whisky. And I don't have to worry about her answering the phone when the school office calls to find out why we are late. Sometimes she stays up late drinking and isn't herself in the morning. "Herself" is the Jeanie Scratch who jumps out of bed to make a thermos of coffee and go surfing. Sometimes I think there are two versions of her.

I search Ms. Chan's face. Her eyes are warm, and she's smiling at us, her hands wrapped around her mug. Cedarveil has some families that rely on fishing or tourism and don't always have the cash for extras, like field trips. Sometimes money is short for families here; sometimes there's more of it. She gets this.

"I understand that, Adelaide. Sometimes I wish I could throw my phone into the ocean," she says with a laugh. "That's why I wanted to talk to your mother in person. Everything's fine, though," she adds, looking at Billy. "We just need to develop some strategies. Get our game plan for some home reading and extra help."

Her black hair is cut into a stylish, shiny blunt cut, and it swings as she talks. Looking at her, remembering how nice she was to me, I become determined not to lie this time.

"My mother can't make it. She's not well. She's not right," I say, talking rapidly, my words charging out like plumes from a whale's blowhole. It's the truth but not the entire truth. Even so, it feels good to say it out loud.

"Oh, I'm sorry to hear that. Maybe we can reschedule for next week."

If Ms. Chan knows I'm not telling the whole story, she doesn't show it. Maybe she will talk to the principal about the no-show. Maybe the principal will call in a social worker. The word *maybe* is always a rabid little dog yapping at my heels.

"That might be a good idea," I say. Then I think of something really smart. "Billy and I can go to the library at lunch to work on his reading."

"Hey!" says Billy, who usually plays "wall ball" with his friends at lunch, which is just some simple game with a tennis ball.

I glare at him. We have to show we are trying. Sometimes I want them all to find out what goes on at Storybook Cabin, how sometimes it's songs and homemade stir-fries and surf talk and bedtime snuggles, and other times it's two kids alone and hungry and scared. When my mother disappears, I can barely sleep. There's never enough to eat. Sometimes I want to tell everyone. I want her to get in trouble. I want a big lunch like Pokey's, with bean soup and crackers, and seaweed salad, and melon and fig bars. Then I feel ashamed that my stomach is so disloyal. I know Mama believes the fridge is full even when it isn't. She just can't see things as they really are sometimes.

"That sounds good, Adelaide. You're so responsible."

I search Ms. Chan's expression to see if she means "in spite of everything" or if she might be planning to call social services. She turns to Billy.

"You might as well take your seat, Billy. The bell's about to ring."

I walk to class, relieved but also disappointed. I don't know how many more times I can get away with this. At least I didn't lie, I tell myself. I am heading down the hall to class, my thoughts thrashing around between wondering where Mama is and worrying about the surfing contest (tomorrow already!) and Billy's reading troubles. Then I remember the muddy, ruined library book still in my backpack. I will have to tell Ms. Cranberg about it. This may be the worst Friday in the history of Fridays.

Pokey and I are lying on the clover-covered hill in the town park situated halfway between the school and the turnoff to the trail that leads to Aerie Beach and our cabin. Sometimes we stop here when we don't feel like going home yet—which for me is often. Billy has tagged along—I keep him close when Mama's gone. He found a friend of his over by the zip line Cedarveil had installed last year as part of an upgrade. As far as I know, the Wisharts didn't pay for that, but who knows. I don't pretend to understand how it all works.

"So you spent lunch at the library?" asks Pokey. He's flipping through some Magic: The Gathering cards. He loves games of all kinds, whether they involve cards, a board or a console.

"Yeah. I helped Billy with his reading. Then I showed Ms. Cranberg the book."

"Oh man," says Pokey, holding a card closer to inspect it. "What'd she say?"

I touch a buttercup growing through the grass. I always think they look like they're nodding off to sleep.

"She asked if I wanted a job shelving books one day a week after school. She said once I'd paid off the book, I could make a little money for the summer. She said she had some kind of fund."

"Well, that's cool," says Pokey.

"Yeah, I guess."

"Hey, wanna come for dinner tomorrow night?" asks Pokey. "My mom's making barbecued chicken. She even said you can sleep over."

Barbecued chicken is one of my favorites, but if I go, Billy will be alone, and I can't tell Pokey that. I dread the day when Pokey and I have to stop having sleepovers—when it seems too weird because he's a boy and I'm a girl.

"Tomorrow's the surf contest," I remind him. "Maybe I'll be too tired for a sleepover."

I love sleeping over at Pokey's house. He has bunk beds, so I usually take the top bunk, or the penthouse, as he calls it. We usually watch a scary movie, and then the next morning his mother makes this egg dish called toad-in-the-hole. Pokey's house makes me happy, but it also makes my heart hurt, because I can see how different his life is. His mom makes all kinds of food, even tempura, and she makes her own bread in a little domed maker. His dad builds things in their garage, like window boxes and stuff. They don't walk to the corner store wearing wetsuit booties. They drive cars and never hitchhike. They not only have phones but also special holders for them in their minivan so they can use them to navigate when they're driving.

Sure, Pokey doesn't get to hear Mama's stories or go surfing in the magic hours of the morning and then have day-old jelly doughnuts and lemon tea. But different can be exhausting.

Pokey snaps a rubber band around his Magic cards. "I'll bet you're just gonna be legend, Addie," he says, in what amounts to an outburst of emotion for him. "I hope you win the contest."

"I do too," I say in a voice that comes out in a squeak.

"Your mom give you any tips?" he asks.

"Sure," I say.

I am legend, all right. I am legend of the half-truth. Mama has given me tips before. And she would if she knew I had entered a surf contest. I'm not even that good. I don't know why I thought I could do it. There's this girl named April, who lives out on the reserve. She's a gnarly surfer, and so is her older sister, May. They're both way better than me. I should have waited and done more training. Now I can't back out. The prize money is too much to ignore. It would make things so much easier and make Mama happier, even just for a bit.

I hate not telling Pokey the whole truth. Now I'm too ashamed. It's as if I've swum so far out, I can't even see the shore anymore.

SATURDAY

I had this idea that I would wake up and my mother would be standing over me, her palm on my forehead, saying, "Hey, little girl, I've missed you, but I'm back now."

Instead I have Billy grabbing me by the shoulders and shaking *me* awake for once.

"Addie, get up. The toilet is making a really funny sound."

It is true. The sound is somewhere between a gurgle and a scream. Mama is really good at fixing stuff around the cabin, which often keeps us from having to bother Mr. Chadawack—or giving him a chance to remind us how much he does for us. Sometimes I think he likes Mama, as if he might ask her to marry him or something, even though he's at least twenty years older than her. Maybe even thirty.

I brush my bangs out of my face and trudge to the bathroom. It smells like a sewer, and the view in the toilet bowl is grisly. I try jiggling the rusty handle, but I know this is a bigger job than that. I kneel on the floor and search for the plunger in the cupboard where we keep our extra toilet paper and laundry soap for when we go to the So Clean. When I reach my hand back to feel for the handle of the plunger, I touch cool round glass. I know without even looking that Mama has hidden one of her empty bottles here. I yelp back a sob, because things may be worse than I'd thought. It's the first time I've found one here. I've found a couple under the kitchen sink. One time I was searching for a sock and found one under her bed.

Billy is standing behind me, waiting, so I blink back tears and try to make my face normal. I find the plunger, fallen down at the very back. I stand up and plunge the toilet twice. My arms are getting stronger—the push-ups are paying off. The clog clears, and the toilet flushes again. I heave a sigh of relief. I am an expert at messes.

I try to push the empty bottle from my mind and go out to the shed to find my wetsuit.

The contest is not at Aerie Beach, *our* beach. It's a forty-minute walk away, at Heinemann Beach. Billy and I retrieve our bikes from the metal shed by the side of the cabin. Our bikes are way too small for us and really embarrassing to look at, so we avoid riding them to school. Wendy Wishart once said my bike wasn't even big enough for her little dog, Tinky. For these reasons, I usually walk. This morning, though, I can't be late.

My insides feel liquefied. I really don't want to do this surf contest. I would rather eat head cheese, a grotesque cold cut that resembles chopped-up fingers. They sell it at the Friendly Cove Deli, where the summer people shop. But it's too late to back out. I have to do it. It's like I'm on a train balanced on the top of a hill, about to come thundering down no matter what.

"Billy, could you please pack up some water? And grab the sunscreen and any food you can find." He nods and ducks back into the cabin. The kid can be super helpful sometimes. Other days he's sulky and makes a whiny sound like a jar full of mosquitos. I check my watch: 8:32 a.m. Billy reemerges with the tin canteens and smiles at me, showing his missing tooth. The morning sun lights the copper highlights in his hair on fire. Mama has the same colors in her hair.

I am inspecting my bike, wondering if I can really ride it all the way to Heinemann. It's at least two sizes too small, and the hot-pink fringe on the handlebars is just humiliating. Billy's bike is red with orange flames on the side. It's not much better. Hopefully, we can get there with no one from school seeing these rides.

"You don't have to come with me," I remind Billy. I don't like to leave him alone, but he won't help my nerves.

"Oh yeah, I do," he says. "Mama's going to show up for sure, don't you think?"

"I don't know, Billy," I say. I don't think I can deal with the surf contest and his disappointment as well. I am secretly crossing my fingers and toes, hoping that somehow she might appear at the last minute and hug me and wish me good luck. But I would never admit that to Billy. I'm feeling far from invincible.

Spring is not the best time to surf in Cedarveil, which is probably why they're holding this new contest now, trying it out before the town gets packed with tourists. The best waves this time of year will probably be wind-swell wedges. Fall brings the early storms to the North Pacific and a good ground swell. Summer brings the visitors and not much in the way of swell—maybe nice gentle rollers for them to learn on, that's what Mama says. She doesn't always like the crowds, but she loves seeing people learn to surf, as if she's handing down a religion. I don't know why she doesn't give surf lessons.

I am debating whether to head back inside and hide under Elizabeth's quilt or get pedaling to Heinemann when I hear the sound of branches snapping along the path. It's Chadawack, wearing his stupid green fleece, khaki shorts, hiking socks and sandals. He's like a cartoon character who wears the same thing every day.

"Your mother here?" he barks by way of greeting.

His eyebrows remind me of two hairy jumping spiders. I saw a photo of them in a book Ms. Cranberg found for me called *Totally Awesome Insects and Spiders*. Those jumping spiders can clear six feet, easy.

"Morning run," says Billy, putting on his bike helmet. He's stuck with my old one, turquoise with My Little Pony on it. Billy doesn't care so much what others say about him, something he gets from Mama.

I wish I were the same, but I can't help it. I even care what Wendy Wishart thinks of me, unfortunately. Billy is getting so good at lying. Mama really does go for early-morning jogs, at least when she hasn't been drinking the night before.

"Well, she's really hardly ever here, is she?" asks Chadawack, in this voice that's always walking the balance beam between hearty-friendly and hostile.

"She's a busy person, Mr. Chadawack," says Billy, smiling a big, toothy grin that I know to be fake. His real smile is a sweet half-moon, lips closed, dimples engaged.

"We'll let her know you stopped by," I say.

"Tell her to stop giving people my phone number. I'm trying to run a business here. People could be phoning about a cottage," he snaps, putting his face right in mine. I see the little red blood vessels on his nose.

"Did someone call for her?" I ask, a bowling ball dropping in my stomach. Phone calls are almost never good. Maybe Grandma Lynn called from Australia. Or maybe the school. Hopefully not the school.

"Something about a job at the whale-watching place," he says. "They want her to call back."

He shoves a piece of paper at me. The letterhead at the top reads *Aerie Beach Cozy Cabins*, and a phone number is scrawled in pencil. Chadawack has terrible handwriting. His letters tangle together like a hairball.

"Thanks," I make myself say. I place the paper in my bike basket, then weigh it down with my water bottle.

Chadawack trundles down the path, leaving us with a view of the thick ropes of veins on the backs of his knees. Billy coughs "hot-dog water" under his breath, and despite it all, I laugh. I tuck my board under my arm and get up on my bike. I guess I'm going to do this thing.

I lock up my bike at the trailhead to Heinemann. My hands are already shaking with nerves. My armpit feels all bruised from where I gripped my board. Billy seems clueless about how jittery I am.

"Taco truck!" he yells, pumping his fist. "You got any money?"

The parking lot is jammed, and there's already a lineup at the food trucks for doughnuts, tacos and coffee. I see girls lined up holding their boards. They're already wearing bright, short-sleeved Lycra shirts over their wetsuits, which must be required for the competition. It starts with teens, and the women compete later in the afternoon.

There are clusters of moms and dads and siblings standing around, the parents clutching their travel mugs of coffee like they're Academy Awards or something. The morning is chilly, as is usual here. When the rest of the island is scorching, the thermometer on the outside wall of our cabin may crack twenty degrees Celsius. It's always colder by the water. The air by the ocean feels like an icy witch breathing spells down your neck.

Seeing all these parents and brothers and sisters gathered together stabs a fork of sadness into my heart. Mama should be here. No, forget that. She should be the one surfing in the contest. Today I don't know if I even like surfing that much. Today I don't know anything except that it's cold and I'm hungry. I pull off my running shoes, realizing I was so nervous that I've forgotten my wetsuit booties. Rookie mistake. I stash my runners by my bike.

"Hey, Adelaide, glad to see you made it. Your heat's coming up soon."

It's Martin, who owns the So Clean Laundromat. Now I really can't back out.

"Hi, Martin," I say. "What are you doing here?"

"I'm a sponsor and also a volunteer now. Actually, my wife voluntold me. Can I mark you present?"

"Yes," I say, smiling at Martin despite the snakes writhing in my belly. Martin used to live in Toronto, and before that, Jamaica. If I run out of quarters at the laundromat, he always spots me for the next week. I hope he doesn't know I'm not thirteen yet.

"Let me just check that we've got all the forms and waivers signed," he says, shuffling through the papers in front of him. I hold my breath. I forged my mother's signature, of course. I took the fifteen-dollar entry fee from her coffee can of emergency money. I think she forgot where she hid it, but I knew it was by the back stoop, near our composter. I'd been saving it for something really, really important—and here it was.

"All looks in order. You better get hopping, Adelaide. They're about to explain the rules."

Martin winks and hands me an orange Lycra jersey to put on, like the other girls. I hate orange, but it's the only one left.

"Good luck!" he calls as I run to the shore with my board under my arm, nearly tripping on my ankle leash. I'm breathing hard when I get there and barely hear the instructions for my age group, which is girls thirteen and fourteen, followed by the fifteen- to sixteen-year-olds and then seventeen-to-eighteen. My heart is pounding in my ears like someone clashing cymbals. I'm going to embarrass myself, Billy, my mother. There are at least fifty people on the beach, ready to watch me fail. I try to focus on the woman in front of me.

"Ladies, welcome to Belle of the Board. I'm Carly, and I'm here to explain the rules. Top two girls from this heat move on to the final and get a chance to win our Belle of the Board prizes. You can also enter our draw to win a stay at the Moon Over Water resort, one of our platinum sponsors."

The young woman telling us this, Carly, has long, straight brown hair and broad shoulders under a fitted hot-pink Lycra top. I can see the outline of her sculpted triceps, and I bet she can really surf. I wonder if my push-ups have done me any good. She's seriously buff.

"We're going to have two heats with four girls in each," she continues, her hands planted on her hips. "There will be an adult helper out in the surf at all times in case anything goes wrong. The heats last twenty minutes, so catch the best waves you can. Our judges will be looking for your form, your speed, your technique and the difficulty of the waves you ride."

The girl at my side is taller than me. She scored the red jersey, a power color. I swallow hard. I hope the contest isn't being live streamed. I don't want anyone to recognize me and know I lied about my age. Martin seems to have no clue, but he's so nice he probably thinks everyone is as good and honest as he is. I scan the beach, looking for Billy. He's stooping down to pet someone's golden retriever. That kid loves dogs. I wave to him, but he doesn't notice, just keeps petting the dog.

I feel alone and exposed. I don't want to surf in front of these people. I glance nervously at the other girls, seeing no familiar faces, maybe because they're all older than me.

"If this goes well, we'll have another, bigger contest in the fall, so get out there and have fun, girls. Your heat starts now!" shouts Carly, pumping her fist in the air.

At that the other three girls in my heat run for the ocean. A seagull lets out a piercing cry, and I begin to run too. As my feet hit the water, I regret not bringing my booties. The water bites into my ankles like a wolf with teeth made of ice. We paddle out, and my heart is already thumping like a bassline.

I am fourth in the line, last in the heat. Under the rules, I take the last turn picking a wave. What were the rest of the rules again? I should have asked my mother more questions about surfing. More questions about my father. More questions about where she goes. About why she can't just stay home with us. A girl at the front of the line with a crown of perfect French braids is about to catch the first wave, a soft roller. She pops up easily, her black braids swinging as she smiles.

"Way to go, Mariko!" someone with lungs calls from the shore.

Next in line is a shorter, stockier girl in a turquoise Lycra top, with thick, strong thighs and a shock of curly, rust-colored hair. She lets a massive wave go by, a big one for spring, and no one muscles in. We're all jumpy, I guess. She has trouble popping up on the next one, positioning her feet too close to the edge of the board.

I need to stop watching and actually do something. My nerves are rolling down a hill and collecting more nerves as they go, a giant dust bunny of anxiety. As the girl in the turquoise top and Mariko paddle back for another go, I am tempted to return to shore and call it all off. The wind is bitter, and my feet are numb. I can't see Billy onshore. Where has he gone?

The adult helper, the one watching over us, high-fives Mariko as she gets back in line. If I go back to shore, the helper will think something is wrong—and I'll have to explain. There is no good way out of this. Also, I really need to pee, which is the worst when you're wearing a wetsuit.

I wait, allowing another wave to go by, and my vision blurs. I'm going to have to make a move soon. Mariko paddles and tries to catch a spilling wave but slips off as she attempts to pop up. I don't think I waxed my board right. I wish my mother was here. Where is Billy?

The turquoise-jersey girl rides a wave for a few seconds, then tumbles into the foam. The wind is picking up, and the swell is increasing. Bailing on this whole thing would be so humiliating. Someone would tell Mama. She'd give me the business for quitting. *What are you made of, girl?* she'd say, her voice full of scorn. But Mama isn't here. She left us. She might not mind that I lied about my age to get in, but she'd go bananas if I quit without trying. Funny, huh? Especially since she quits us on a regular basis.

I suddenly feel like screaming, screaming *to* her, screaming *at* her. Why does she always have to go?

Then I come back to myself, like a cartoon genie sucked into a bottle. A hollow wave is coming, and I know it is meant for me. I have to do *something*. I paddle, my arms dipping into the cold, gray water. I pop up quick. I am standing right in the heart of the wave, and I pivot, like my mother showed me. I hear a roaring, either in my head or from the wave. The peak is above my head. I almost smile as I try to carve again.

I look out at the face of the wave, and I wish my mother could see me. It's the biggest wave I've taken on. I bend my knees and try to steady myself, but the peak of the wave is closing over me like a curling fist. I realize I am going to fall, and I try to jump away from my board, over the wave.

"Cover your head!" I hear a woman call, so I do as I tumble into the foam. The voice sounds like Mama's, I think, as the sound is snuffed out and my vision goes gray.

THE WASHING MACHINE

Picture a girl lying on the sand, her palms upturned. The waves wash over her, as if the sea is trying to snatch her back in. If this were a Disney movie, she'd be a mermaid with long, flowing hair, who has a dancing red crab as her sidekick. In the movie, she'd lose her voice in a bad bargain with a sea witch.

But this is real life. The girl is a real girl. Her whole body has been scrubbed with salt water, inside and out. Her lungs burn, and the side of her right foot weeps like a raw, red tomato where it dragged against a rock. She tries to scream but instead groans into a puddle of salt water. Her body is as limp and boneless as a strand of kelp. Hands are grabbing her now, towing her farther up the beach. She hears a familiar voice, saying "Adelaide, Adelaide!"

My eyes focus again, and I look into two kind brown eyes. The woman is wearing glasses, but they are covered in droplets of water from the ocean. I try to take a gasp of air, and I make a wheezing sound like a deflating balloon.

"Adelaide," I hear again. A soft, cold hand is holding mine.

"Please stand back, ma'am," comes another voice, a man's, from my other side.

"Ms. Cranberg?" I ask. She is standing over me, and I realize she is wearing a wetsuit. She must be one of the volunteers in the water. This idea shocks me for a second. I had no idea that she surfed.

"You sure gave us a scare, Adelaide," she says. "I'll go find your mom."

If only she could. If only there were a book: *How to Find Your Mother*.

"These paramedics are going to examine you, and then we'll head to the hospital. You were underwater for a few seconds."

"No hospital," I say, my voice coming out in a croak. Hospitals have forms and social workers and questions to be answered.

"These nice people are going to get you warmed up, make sure your neck and spine are okay. I'll go find your mom."

No you won't, I think.

"Can you find Billy?" I ask, and suddenly I am so, so tired. Pokey was supposed to come watch me surf. Now I hope he stayed home, even though he always makes me feel better.

The paramedic drapes two fleece blankets around me, and I think how nice it is to have someone tuck me in.

"That was some wave—good on ya," he says. He sounds Australian, that twangy accent. "Ya got a ride in the washing machine, though."

I realize he is right. I got rolled underwater by a wave. The paramedic probably surfs. Lots of the year-round people here started out as visitors, but they stay because they live to surf. I wonder if the paramedic knows my mother. He looks young and has an ear cuff on one lobe. If he's part of the local surf scene, he's likely heard of her—mad Jeanie Scratch.

"You're going to be just fine, just ripper," he says. "Can I take a peep at your blood pressure?"

I nod yes, holding out my arm.

"My dad is Australian," I say, and I close my eyes, still hearing the pounding sound of the surf and the crowd cheering the other girls on.

When I open my eyes, I see Billy, Ms. Cranberg and Pokey standing over me. I wonder if I am dreaming, because this is such a random assortment of people. Then I remember the surf contest.

"Well, that didn't go like you expected," says Pokey, peering at me.

"Addie, that wipeout was positively savage," says Billy.

I groan. My body aches. I want to get out of the wetsuit and into my blue-striped flannel pajamas. I want to get under Elizabeth's heavy, warm quilt and never get out of bed again, forget I ever entered this contest. I'm done with trying, period.

"We were worried about you," says Pokey. He never hides his feelings, just brings them to the light like ornaments made of blown glass. I suddenly remember the glass float, still sitting on the kitchen table. We forgot to take it to the antique shop.

Billy has picked up my hand. He hardly ever holds my hand, except when we are watching the scariest of movies at the Paradise Theater in town. He held my hand during *Infinity War* (which we snuck into), but only during the very saddest part.

"You're in the first-aid tent," says Ms. Cranberg. "We're keeping you warm while we try to reach your mom. Is she at work today?"

"I don't know," I say, because I can't think of the correct lie fast enough. It's like trying to find the right lid for a jar. The wrong lie can really sink your battleship.

"My mom can take her home," says Pokey. "She just drove me over to watch Addie's heat. She's waiting in the parking lot."

I wonder what Pokey would say if he knew I sometimes find empty bottles in the cabin. Or if he knew how many nights I've lain awake listening for the creak of a door, fearing a burglar but hoping it was Mama.

"I'd really feel better if I could talk to your mom, Adelaide," says Ms. Cranberg. "Hey, Pokey, Billy, can you go buy us all hot chocolate?"

She hands Pokey a ten-dollar bill, and they shuffle out. Someone has placed thick, black wool socks on my feet. I look up at the fabric ceiling of the tent. It is black, too, like the night sky. I know this is not about hot chocolate.

"Listen, Adelaide," she says in a whoosh of words. "The first-aid guys are out there, waiting. But I wanted to say to you that I know you're going to be all right. Not just now, but in general. You're so smart and brave. I heard about how you saved Evie Wishart."

"You did?" I had kind of forgotten about that. My brain gets really full sometimes.

She nods. "A lot of people heard about it. I have to ask you a very important question, though, and I really need the truth."

I swallow. I know what's coming, and my eyes prick with tears.

"Do you know where your mother is today? Has she left you and your brother alone?"

Ms. Cranberg's voice is shaking, and I realize she didn't want to ask the question. She's been my favorite thing about school, and now I have to lie to her. I know once I tell the lie, I will never be able to look at her the same. I can never go back. When she finds me a book, or asks me how a school project is going, I will remember that I lied to her.

But if I don't lie, Mama will get in trouble. And maybe we'll be sent away, like Elizabeth. We'd have to leave Cedarveil and Pokey. We'd have to make new friends. We'd even have to make new enemies. The thought drains the last of my energy. I curl my toes up in the socks. The wool makes the bottom of my feet itch.

Mama's always been one to take risks when surfing, not afraid to face the biggest, gnarliest waves. It's hard to believe someone so brave can also be so beaten down. I think of how Pokey once asked if my mother had just had dental surgery, because she was tripping over her tongue and couldn't say the phrase *cinnamon toast* when she was offering us a snack. She'd clearly been drinking before we came home from school. I was never sure what I'd find if Mama was home. It was like opening a picnic basket and not knowing if you were going to find it filled with green apples or green snakes. Last month I bit my nails down so far down that it hurt to hold a basketball.

"I could sure use that hot chocolate," I say, stalling. "I'm sure I'll be fine after that."

Ms. Cranberg stares at me. "Adelaide, I'm on your side."

I ball up my fists, because I'm about to cry. I have so much to say, so many different stories to tell, like the time my mother fell off her bike in front of the school, and Wendy Wishart saw and laughed.

That was before my mother's bike got stolen from the beach. Or how she wrote the lyrics to an entire song called "The Ballad of Adelaide Scratch" and had Martin write the music for it. When she's home, she still sings the song to me. Who else has a mother who writes them their own song?

Just then Pokey and Billy return, each holding two paper cups. Ms. Cranberg frowns at them for a second, but I'm the only one who notices. She doesn't have her answer yet. Part of me is annoyed at her for asking, for reminding me that I could have a different kind of life, with a different kind of mother. I inhale. Billy, I think. I could not live without Billy. It's an icicle-sharp thought.

"My mom wanted to be here. You know she wouldn't miss anything to do with surfing. But she had an interview to work at the whale-watching company. The summer rush is coming up, you know. They need extra people."

Ms. Cranberg tilts her head, breathes out the air she was holding in.

"Oh yeah," says Billy, holding out a steaming cup to Ms. Cranberg. "Mama really wants that job."

I feel a burning in my chest, like the breakfast I barely ate is going to come up. Billy is far too good at lying. And I am too.

"Well, I do hope she gets it, then," says Ms. Cranberg quietly.

Can it ever be the same once you've lied to someone? I've lied to Mr. Chadawack so many times, but I don't like him. This is different.

Adelaide Scratch, named for a coastal town,
Oh, she'll always lift you up, but she'll never let you down.
She's as beautiful as fire and as wise as a star.
I'll always love you, Adelaide, wherever you are.

Those are the lyrics to the chorus, in case you were wondering.

THE BELLE OF THE BOARD

I don't even know who won the surf contest. It seems so silly that I thought I might win. It hurts to hope sometimes. It makes my skin sting, like my whole body has windburn.

I am cleared to go by the paramedics, so Mrs. Polk offers to drive Billy and me home, or as close to home as she can. You can't drive right to our cabin door, so it tends to keep visitors away, except for Mr. Chadawack, who trots down from the main office or his own cabin in his ridiculous socks and sandals.

"Your mother will be worried sick when she finds out," says Mrs. Polk, lifting up the hatch of her minivan to put our bikes in the back, followed by my surfboard. Mrs. Polk has a cheery array of bright fleece jackets. Today's is pink, which she has paired with jeans, Hunter boots and a white crocheted cap.

"She really should get a cell phone," she adds before shutting the van door.

Mrs. Polk is not the only one to forget that smartphones don't grow from people's wrists and that they cost money. She doesn't mean to be unkind, so I just let it go.

"May I have another scone?" asks Billy, from his spot in the middle of the back seat. He loves riding in the Polk minivan. A soft rain starts up, sprinkling the windows, which makes it seem cozy.

"Of course, honey, but I don't want to spoil your lunch," she chirps, buckling up and turning on the radio. If only she knew. I can't remember what we have left in the fridge. Maybe I can palm an extra scone for later.

"I sure hope she gets that job," says Mrs. Polk, too cheerfully. She knows my mother isn't typical. But she doesn't know the whole story, and I'm not sure she wants to. If she ever found out, she might not let me be friends with Pokey.

"Me too," I say, forcing my voice to sound bright. "I mean, it would be great for her to have another job."

"I'll bet you do a lot around the house," says Mrs. Polk, tapping her fingers on the steering wheel to the pop song on the radio.

I watch trees roll by, a blur of green in the rain. Then Mr. Soong's gas station, where the big RVs stop to buy their ice on their way to Rocky Point National Park. There's a rule at that park that you can't leave any food out, not even a bottle of barbecue sauce, because it draws the cougars, wolves and bears. Last year a wolf took one of the tourist's dogs right from a busy hiking trail. *Poof!* Gone. The wolf wasn't trying to be mean. It just knew it was hungry.

"I guess," I say, hugging myself. I am still cold from being in the water. I changed out of my wetsuit, and Ms. Cranberg lent me sweats to wear home. The sweatshirt is a soft, light blue and says *UBC* on it, for University of British Columbia. It's fleecy and warm. I like to think I could go to university one day, maybe to study marine biology. The pants are way too big, so I fold up the waistband to try to make them smaller.

"Pokey," I say, to change the subject. "Did you know that because of global warming, sharks are being seen in our waters?"

I sound like I've just delivered a line in a nature documentary. I stare down at the scone in my fist and squeeze it, showering crumbs on the sweatshirt. Then, for some embarrassing reason, I start to cry. Luckily, no one notices.

There is silence in the van as the trees hum by and we get closer to Cedarveil. We pass the food bank, someplace I'll bet the Polks only visit to volunteer, sorting cans.

"Addie," asks Pokey, in his slow, careful way. "Are you afraid of sharks?"

"I think she's worried *for* the sharks," offers Billy. He has a smudge of flour on his cheek from the scone.

I decide that I am too exhausted to talk anymore, so we spend the rest of the ride listening to the radio. When we get to our lane, I wave away Mrs. Polk's offer of help to schlep our bikes and my surfboard. In fact, the offer makes me angry. How does she think we got them out of there? Then I feel bad for getting angry, because she is just being kind.

I wave to Pokey and his mom, and as they pull away the rain starts falling harder. As we walk back to the cabin, sword ferns slap at my legs. I feel I deserve that, somehow, having been several flavors of stupid. Entering the contest, thinking I could win, having a spectacular wipeout.

Billy and I set our bikes at the side of the cabin—they're already rusty—but I carry the helmets and my surfboard to the shed, like I've been taught. Mama can be pretty loose on tidiness, but she says you should always put away your board when you're done surfing. And I am definitely done. I am going to take a hot shower and read my library books under the covers until the world seems better.

MONDAY HAPPENS, AGAIN

Sunday is stormy, with howling wind. I spend most of it in the cabin, working on a school project about ancient Egypt. The best thing about the day is that Billy found a baggie of leftover Halloween candy in our junk drawer, so we divvy it up and eat it while reading. Billy pages through a Captain Underpants book and snort-laughs in between licks of his Tootsie Pop, so he is enjoying those things, at least. We go to bed jittery from sugar and food coloring, our bellies still rumbling for real food. I lie in bed dreaming of a fat roast-beef sandwich with lettuce, honey mustard and a dill pickle.

I also crave a Caesar salad, of all things. I don't usually like them, but for some reason I want the crunchy lettuce and creamy dressing.

I turn over and over, trying to sleep, but I'm too hungry, and I can't stop thinking about the surf contest, Ms. Cranberg, the feeling of being underwater. I think I haven't slept at all, that I've stayed up all night, when I hear Billy shouting into my ear.

"Wake up, Addie, it's eight o'clock! We're going to be late!"

I fly out of bed and sprint to the bathroom, stopping to remove a Mr. Big wrapper stuck to my bare foot. We. Cannot. Be. Late. We rush out the door, our teeth unbrushed. We look unmade, unmothered, and my hair is tangled up like kelp in a crab trap. It is not a good day. We are so late that we have to do something awful: take our dinky, embarrassing bikes.

"Your helmet," I croak to him, handing him the My Little Pony humiliation generator.

He nods and clips it on. We start pedaling, speeding up as we pass by Chadawack's line of mushroom-shaped cabins. He's the last person we want to see.

Pokey is not at his usual station, having no doubt given up on us and walked ahead to school. My backpack flaps against me, light. I forgot to make us lunch, I realize as we pass through town, almost to school. Billy pedals behind me. It's not raining at least, and a crack of sunshine is poking through the mashed-potato clouds. *Ugh, everything reminds me of food.*

I roll up along the sidewalk to the So Clean Laundromat, nearly mowing down Martin, who is standing out front with a mug of coffee in one hand and a ceramic plate in the other.

"Adelaide!" he calls. "Slow down and try my salt-fish fritters!"

I stop, plant my feet and smile, despite myself. He hands Billy and me each one, wrapped in a paper napkin. The fritters are crispy and hot, with tiny bits of green onion in them.

"Thank you," I say, chewing. I tuck the rest of the fritter in my bike basket for later. Billy mumbles his thanks, his mouth full. I wave and keep pedaling, stopping only to check for traffic, remembering the close call with Evie.

Our tires hit school property with three minutes to spare before the bell goes.

"We did it," I say to Billy. All we have to do is stash our bikes at the rack behind the school, where fewer people will see them. There will be no phone calls home and no detentions.

I hop off my bike and start walking it around back, motioning for Billy to do the same. I'm tempted to risk it getting stolen—but then I'd have no ride at all. It seems I've pulled off another Monday morning. My Egypt project is done, and I can eat the fritter Martin gave me. I might get through the day.

I pass a cluster of kids, including Wendy, gathered near the statue of A.F. Fenston, who is this old, bald guy who founded the town of Cedarveil. Lots of people have a hate on for the statue, including me, because really, Indigenous people were in this neck of the woods first, and the guy just ran a logging company. Fenston was a short man to boot, but the statue is on a tall platform.

Then, instead of the school bell, I hear a burst of tinny music from a phone, followed by the sound of laughing and the words "*Wipe out!*" I know the song. It's an old one from the 1960s, by the Surfaris. My mother has played it on her stereo.

Then I hear an outburst of real, actual laughter.

"It's totally her!" someone says.

"She's not such a big hero now," I hear Wendy say.

Everyone's looking at one phone. It has a hot-pink case with black polka dots, which means it belongs to Wendy. Then my knees turn to pudding, and I know what it is, what has happened. It's my wipeout from the contest. Someone with a phone captured it on video.

It takes me two seconds to figure out who it was. Wendy. The Wisharts' resort was a sponsor. She must have been there. Tears spring to my eyes, and I consider hopping on my pink mess of a bike and pedaling away to anywhere. But my Egypt project is due, and half my class has already seen me there. I don't know why Wendy hates me so much. Or maybe she's just mean. Maybe she doesn't care either way, and she's like those spiders and snakes in Australia, stinging and biting because it's all they know.

"Show me," I say to Pokey when we meet at lunch. "Wait. No, don't." I had asked him earlier to find it on his phone. He's seen it.

"It's not that bad, really," he says, and I hear that laughter again from the beginning of "Wipe Out." Couldn't she find a newer song?

I still can't look. I've never seen a video of me surfing, and I don't want this to be the first.

"I think it makes you look cool," says Pokey, stopping to scratch his knee. He's got a Darth Vader T-shirt on, just in case it doesn't feel enough like Monday.

"Where did she post it?" I ask with a feeling of dread. I suddenly feel self-conscious that I am wearing the same green T-shirt I wore to bed.

"On the Wisharts' resort blog page. I guess they were sponsors? There were other videos too."

"But only one epic wipeout," I add.

"Maybe," concedes Pokey.

Over by the Wishart jungle gym, Wendy is now holding up her polka-dot phone for a new group of kids. This time she's cornered the cast of this year's musical as they were trying to run their lines. I probably should have tried out for *The Wizard of Oz*. People tell me I have a nice singing voice. Sometimes, even though I am only eleven, I feel that life is passing me by.

The chords of "Wipe Out" blare in my direction, and I can't wait for lunch—and this day—to end. I start to think about what to do for getting food. After school Billy and I could ride our bikes down the back alleys of the cafés to check the dumpsters. There are sometimes cold, burned pizzas behind DeMarco's Pies. If not, we'll have to keep looking. Pokey will be walking home anyway. I won't have to make an excuse.

Picture a Girl

Part of me wants to march over to Wendy, shove her in the chest and ask her why she's so mean. But I stay frozen, seated, on the bench next to Pokey. Just then Billy's class files past, on their way to the Cedarveil library for their field trip. Billy waves at me, a big grin on his face.

"Your video is awesome," the boy next to him in line calls to me. It's one of the DuMoulin boys. I forget his name. They all have red hair and freckles. The DuMoulin boy gives me the hang-ten sign.

"My sister has nerves of steel," says Billy. "Nothing scares her." He waves again as Ms. Chan hurries him to catch up to the group.

"Well, that's another way of looking at it," says Pokey. "Do you want to see the video now?"

I nod. It only lasts a few seconds, but I am struck by how tall I am now. And then yes, one spectacular wipeout, my board flying, a churning blur of limbs and waves. The video cuts out after that, so my rescue remains a mystery.

"Wendy must have been on the shore," says Pokey, taking back his phone. "It's pretty easy to stay on the sidelines and criticize."

He holds out a tub of tomato-basil rice cakes for me to take some. I love Pokey. He's wise beyond his years and generous with his snacks. He often brings an extra tub of his mom's seaweed salad just for me. I crunch a rice cake, then walk over to the statue of Fenston. I circle around the back, assessing it. Fenston did nothing really noteworthy, probably never put a meal on the table in his life, just clear-cut some trees to make a name for himself.

I assess the slope, and then I climb onto the platform and shimmy up to the very top of his bald head. I am poised there on one leg as the playground starts to take notice. No one has ever climbed to the top of the statue before.

The whole playground is watching to see what I will do. This is totally counter to my usual practice of hiding and blending in. I have nothing left to lose.

I jump, raising my arms as I land and hit the ground in my cheap sneakers, like a gymnast completing a routine. *Fump!* Shocked silence and then a smattering of applause. It was a near-perfect dismount.

There. I did something else besides that wipeout. This will give them a new thing to think about. The bell rings, and we file back into the school, Pokey regarding me with silent amazement.

We turn to walk back to class, but first I ask Pokey if I can borrow his phone. He looks puzzled but hands it over.

"I just want to send an email," I say.

It's an easy one to remember. I type quickly, and then it's off with a *whoosh*.

Billy and I are almost home when I remember that we forgot to scan the town dumpsters for food. Part of me is relieved, because I hate doing it—the stench, the fear of someone seeing us or—worst of all—the prospect of finding a rodent. We will have to scrounge in the cupboards. Again. Billy has been going on and on about my awesome surf video. I may have lost face with the sixth grade, but I am killing it with the third graders. Apparently with them you don't actually have to be skilled—being bold is enough.

"Skylar Maldonado wants to go surfing with you sometime," Billy says as we roll up to the cabin. This makes me laugh.

"What? He wants to see me wipe out again? No thanks."

When I open the shed to put away the bikes, I see a gap in all our piles of crap—the croquet set we found at the Sally Ann, our rusted garden spade, a Coleman stove we use during power outages. I scan the shed, and then I realize what is missing—her surfboard, aka Joan Jett. I am sure the board was there this morning.

"Billy," I say, backing out of the shed.

"Yeah, what?"

"She's back."

Billy pauses for a second, then turns and sprints down the trail, making a lightning bolt for the beach. I stop for a second, thump my chest once with my fist as if I am restarting my heart, then run after him. I am filled with anger at her—for going surfing instead of searching us out. For leaving us for seven days and six nights. For making me wonder, every night, if she was alive or dead. Because I was nearly swallowed by the sea, and she wasn't here. And I don't regret sending that email. But I run, because I am hungry for the sight of her.

I crash through the forest, wearing my thin, secondhand Nikes that get heavy with mud. I don't want Billy to beat me to her, but he got a head start. I tumble onto Aerie Beach, and there she is, her wetsuit a black dot out on the churning gray water. Billy is right by the shore, watching her, waving so hard his arm might fly away like a boomerang.

I stand, waiting for her to glide into view, the wet sand soaking into the holes in my shoes. Out in the surf is the only place my mother ever truly feels comfortable, I realize, watching her. If they could put that feeling in a bottle, she would drain it dry.

I already know what she's going to say to us. *Hello, grommets, how I've missed you so!*

It's the same thing every time.

Suddenly I can't bear to hear it. I turn around and walk back into the woods, leaving Billy waiting for her. Maybe she was in Campbell River or Vancouver, or maybe she's been in Peru.

I only know the one place that she wasn't.

Here.

THE LISTENING TREE

I sit under Crooked Red, letting the rain drench my clothes and cover my face. I feel more alone than ever. I pat the roots of the big tree, and they feel like a bony hand.

"Sometimes I think she wishes she hadn't had us," I say, glancing up as a kingfisher flits by. I don't mind a bird eavesdropping.

"She says we are the best thing that ever happened to her, but then she leaves us with no food. That's not normal! What if something happened to Billy? I'm just a kid."

I let that thought hang there. I feel like Crooked Red is nodding its branches. I have never had a real heart-to-heart with Crooked Red before, never felt like talking. I can't mention the drinking, not even to Crooked Red. It makes me so anxious, not knowing what's going to happen next. Sometimes not knowing what will happen next is a good feeling, like when you can't wait to turn a page in a book. But sometimes it's bad. Often, for me, it's bad.

"I'm really upset I had to lie to Ms. Cranberg," I say.

I really liked working in the library. It made me feel that I had a purpose besides trying to look after Billy, which wasn't really my job in the first place.

The rain slows, and a gentle wind rustles Crooked Red's leaves. I wonder if the tree is really magic. It seems unlikely. Still, I am glad Mama saved it. Sometimes she can be so strong. I wonder why she needs her medicine. I try to remember back to when she didn't drink—but I can't. It's as if the past two years have fogged the mirror, and I can't see what came before.

"I feel like if I try harder, I can get her to stop, I can get her to stay," I say to Crooked Red, my hand still on its root, which is cold and smooth. I say the words, but they don't seem true to me. I don't really believe I can get her to stop. I smell the cedar and the salt air, plus something else. The licorice smell of wild fennel. I stop and listen for footsteps and hear a seagull cry. Nothing else.

"I *am* angry with her," I say to Crooked Red. "None of it is fair."

Mama's not coming to look for me. Maybe Billy and I both dreamed her out there on the sea. My heart beats faster, like someone's whacking my chest with a mallet. Maybe she got caught in a rip tide and didn't come in.

No, Mama's a survivor.

I sigh. My chest still burns a little from taking in all that salt water at the contest.

"I wish she would teach me how to really surf," I say.

I still want to see her, despite everything. I still want to *be* like her, despite everything. I stand up, my legs wobbly. I've turned to head back to the trail when I see her standing there, waiting. She is wearing her Helly Hansen rain jacket, the one that makes her blue eyes pop.

"Hi," she says softly.

I hear a raindrop plop from the tree to the mossy ground. I become aware that I am starving, my body a train that chugs on with or without a conductor. I turn away from her, not ready to talk.

"I thought you'd be here," she says, standing on the very path those men had to make around Crooked Red. Her black gumboots are planted on the boardwalk. She knows not to come any closer right now.

"You don't know anything about me," I say, my anger cracking through my determination not to speak. "You don't even know what happened this week. I could have been dead for all you know. Billy could have been dead."

We let that statement hang there in the quiet of the forest. That will sting her, and I am glad.

"I missed you," she says, in her typical way of diverting from things she doesn't want to talk about.

I know this is true. I also know it is not enough.

"Where were you?" I ask, my tone bitter. I vowed not to talk to her, but my rage is bubbling over. There is a poison in me that I need to spit out.

"On the mainland," she says. "Hanging out with some old friends. I needed a break."

"A break from what?" I sob, turning to her. "Are we so bad?"

She stares at me, her eyes filling with tears. Her face clouds over with something else: shame. "I needed a break from myself, Adelaide, not you."

I nod, snuffling. I want to tell her that I sometimes find her empty bottles. That she doesn't hide them very well. That I *know*.

"Mama," I say, trying out her name again. Part of me can't believe she is back. I have been dreaming of her return. But having her leave again is more than I can take. I might snap in two, like a surfboard smashed on the rocks. Half of me loves Mama more than anyone, and the other half wants her to leave for good, forever, and not put us through this anymore.

"Yes, grommet?"

She still isn't moving any closer to me.

"Do you think you could maybe call Grandma Lillian? I miss her."

Mama frowns at this. She wasn't expecting that. Grandma Lillian and Mama are always feuding about something. She doesn't live that far away, but we haven't seen her since Easter of last year. Mama was stubbornly set on baking a ham, and that was nothing but bad news. Our wonky oven burns brownies at the best of times. The ham was scorched in some places and undercooked in others, and Grandma Lillian can be critical. Mama had started refilling her own wineglass before it was empty. Grandma Lillian had just sipped her tea and scowled.

I decide to swallow my anger and be careful.

"I miss Grandma," I say. "You two get along sometimes. Can't she come visit?"

This is true. They run hot and cold. Grandma Lillian thinks surfing is a waste of time, which is one sticking point (and that's like saying a rhino's horn is a sticking point). And Grandma Lillian also used to drink—or so Mama says—but now she doesn't at all. She once told me she wants Mama to quit too. And Mama doesn't like to be told what to do, by anyone. That is a big part of the problem. What I don't mention is that I already emailed Grandma Lillian, using Pokey's phone, and asked her to come for a visit. I didn't say Mama was gone. I just said we hoped she would visit soon. That we really needed her here. That *I* needed her here.

"I will consider it," says Mama stiffly. "If that is what you and Billy want."

"It is," I say, trying not to snuffle. I am now cold as well as hungry.

"Now can I give you a hug?" she asks.

No one gives a tighter hug than Mama. She can squeeze the breath right out of you, pressing her fingers into your back. When I hug her, she feels thinner than when she left. Her embrace is what

I've been dreaming of, but I don't want to let her off the hook again.

"Mama, we'd better go. Billy doesn't like to be alone for too long," I say, as if she's forgotten what her own son does and doesn't like.

She just nods, choosing to ignore my rebuke. She takes my hand. We say nothing as we walk to the cabin, but she squeezes my hand hard. When I push the door open, it squeaks as usual.

"Addie," says Billy. "Guess what? Mama brought sushi!"

He's already sitting at the green kitchen table, his eyes shining. He has laid out our heavy plates, gray-blue, and poured glasses of lemonade. He has set down forks, because Billy isn't good with chopsticks. I am still angry, but Billy is so excited that I cannot ruin it for him. He loves sushi, and so do I—and Mama knows it.

"I got extra wasabi," she says, reaching for the container on the table. We may not have groceries for tomorrow, but we have food now. "My friend Sara set me up with some landscaping work in Vancouver. Lots of big gardens. I can pay some bills."

I try not to roll my eyes. There are landscaping jobs here too. She didn't have to go so far away to pull weeds for rich people. We have both those things right here.

"Tell me what you've been doing, grommets," says Mama. As if it's a normal thing for a mom to just disappear for several days, then come back with no explanation and a few extra packs of wasabi.

"Well, Adelaide was in a surf contest. And was doing awesome. Then she had this savage wipeout!"

"What?" asks Mama, sitting down in her chair. No one else sat in Mama's chair when she was away. We only have three chairs, even though there's space for four. One broke a year ago, and we moved it out by the shed instead of getting it repaired. It looks as if she's sticking with lemonade tonight, which makes my shoulders relax. It even appears she's brought some food for breakfast as well. There are a loaf of bread and a bunch of bananas on the counter.

"It was nothing. I'm okay," I say. "But I could use some surf lessons."

"I can do that," says Mama.

I tear the paper from the chopsticks and lift up a California roll to my mouth. Suddenly it seems like years since I've eaten.

"Mama," I ask, chewing. "Can I tell the story tonight? I've been practicing."

It's true. I have been telling this story to myself over and over. It is time to share. She pauses, her chopsticks hovering over a puddle of soy sauce on her plate. She frowns, a crease between her blue eyes.

"That's usually my job," she says. "But just for tonight."

THE
STORYBOOK CABIN

"Picture a girl. Her name is Annie. She's eleven years old and lives in a cabin set in a wild green patch of woods by the sea. The Storybook Cabin is a place where stories are made and told, put together word by word, in much the same way that a bricklayer builds a house. Sometimes the stories are happy and sometimes very sad, so sad your heart might snap in two like a chopstick.

"The girl lived a lucky kind of life in some ways—she had a younger brother named Bobby and a loyal friend and a mama who was usually there—but not always. Sometimes Mama disappeared for days on end, and during those times life was not easy for Bobby and Annie.

"The girl had troubles, like everyone. For example, she had a sworn enemy at school named Wanda Meanhart, but usually, with some help from her friends, Annie could keep out of Wanda's way.

"One day Annie woke up to go to school, and she was so hungry. Super extra supremely hungry. She opened the fridge to find only a glass jar of dill water—with no pickles left—a half carton of milk and some old horseradish that should have galloped away a long time ago. And who wants horseradish for breakfast?

"'I'm hungry,' said Bobby, who had just woken up.

"'Me too,' said Annie. She might have grown three inches overnight, and now she was so hungry that she could have eaten a bobcat—provided that the bobcat was made of grilled cheese or chocolate layer cake.

"Annie realized then that her mother was not in her bed, not in the kitchen and not in the bathroom. Annie was on her own, with no grown-ups to help, and if she and Bobby were going to eat that day, she would have to steal, or make magic, or win some kind of bet. Their home was on Better's Bay, after all. She walked down to the beach to consider her options, Bobby trailing after her. They sat down on a wet cedar log while she pondered. Right then a sea witch with frosty white skin, black teeth, gold eyes and green hair burst up from the sea. She had a croaky, grating voice, much like a foghorn.

"'Are you hungry, children two? I know just what you can do. Lend me a voice to put in my jar. I'll keep it close—it won't go far. I want a chance to try to sing. In return I'll bring you a table full of wondrous dishes. Anything your hungry heart wishes.'

"Bobby looked at Annie. Annie looked at Bobby. It seemed legit. They were both starving. Besides, she'd get her voice back, right?

"'Okay,' said Annie. 'You can take my voice, but you have to return it.'

"'Right,' said Bobby, slapping his knees, no doubt excited at the mountain of food. 'It's just a loaner. You can meet again at dusk.'

"'Deal,' said the sea witch, raising a foamy limb instead of offering a handshake. Then she sprung out her claws, reached into Annie's throat and ripped out her voice.

"Annie and Bobby went back to the cabin, where they found the magical feast waiting. There were plates piled high with strips of grilled bacon, blueberry pancakes, three kinds of melon and cups of hot chocolate with marshmallows bobbing on top like life preservers. Annie opened the fridge and found the shelves stacked with containers of different types of sushi—salmon, tuna and little rolls filled with vegetables. Annie and Bobby hardly ever had sushi—it was kind of expensive—but the sea witch knew they both dreamed of it. Annie shut the fridge door, saving the sushi for later, and rushed to sit down at the table.

"'I like ham better,' said Bobby before grabbing a piece of bacon with his fingers.

"Annie just nodded, because she couldn't speak. After a few minutes of frenzied eating, she was full, and she wanted to say how good the food was, but she could only rub her belly. While she puttered around the cabin and washed the plates, she wanted to sing to herself, but she couldn't because her voice was gone. Bobby lay on the couch, snoring, with his hands resting on his full belly. Annie was sleepy too, but her worries kept her awake.

"As the sky darkened, casting shadows over the cabin, Annie began to wonder if she'd made a bad deal. She glanced at the kitchen clock. Soon it would be dusk—time to meet the sea witch.

"Bobby was still asleep, so Annie walked the trail to the beach on her own, wearing a T-shirt, jean shorts and her rain boots. A light rain was falling, and she watched her yellow boots traveling down the path, which was covered in cedar leaves and pine needles. Branches scratched her bare legs, but she couldn't cry out.

"She was alone on Aerie Beach, and the wind chilled her bare arms. She should have worn a jacket. She clenched her fists, digging her fingernails into her palm to make little half-moons. She waited, watching the waves break. A seal bobbed by, raising its puppy-dog face to her, twitching its whiskers. Annie wanted to say hello, but she couldn't. The air just scraped in her throat, making no sound at all. She waited and waited, as the sky got darker and the waves smacked against the rocks. Annie waited there until the sky was black and the bats came out and the stars winked behind the fog. Annie held her elbows and shivered.

"Then she knew. The sea witch was never coming back. Annie had been tricked. She walked home, stumbling in the dark and crying silent sobs. She couldn't even cry properly anymore.

"Bobby was awake when she returned home. Seeing her tears, he gave her a hug. It was past dinnertime, so they ate the sushi in the fridge and slept side by side in their mother's bed for comfort. The magic food was now gone. When they woke in the morning, the kitchen table was littered with empty sushi containers—nothing left but small globs of wasabi and rivers of soy sauce. They had no food for breakfast, and they were going to be late for school."

"Addie," says Mama, in a quavering warning tone.

She wants this to be a fun time. Her homecoming. I shouldn't spoil things. But what if it had been Billy who had run in front of the car instead of Evie, and I hadn't been there? She could have come home and Billy would have been gone forever. Did she even think about that? Does she even think about us when she's gone?

"Let me finish," I say. Billy's eyes are wide, but I keep talking.

"Annie and Bobby hurried to school, their bellies growling like black bears protecting a berry patch. They walked in silence except for the sound of their boots squelching in the mud. Annie realized that she had lost something important just to get something else that many kids had and took for granted. It seemed unfair. It *was* unfair. Annie wanted to howl, but the howl stayed trapped in her chest like a Tasmanian devil.

"Annie and Bobby split up to go to their classrooms, Annie waving goodbye. When the teacher called her to spell *Saskatchewan*, Annie had to shrug and pretend she didn't know the answer. How could she explain that she'd been tricked by a sea witch into giving so much away?

"'What a dummy,' said Wanda Meanhart. 'She can't surf, and she can't spell.'"

"Wendy Wishart said you can't surf?" Mama interrupts, her hand gripping her lemonade glass.

"I never interrupt your stories," I point out. Mama hates when people interrupt her stories.

"That's true," says Billy, who is so happy to have Mama home that his face is glowing.

I've ruined our perfect night—the sushi, the story time. She's angry. I think of how I had to lie to Ms. Cranberg. How I had to fight my way back up from under that wave.

"And that's it. End of story," I say.

Billy looks confused now, like he doesn't understand at all. I stand up, my chair scraping the floor. I walk to the cabin door, without knowing what I'm doing or where I'm going to go.

"Don't you leave, Adelaide Elizabeth Scratch," says Mama, waving her finger at me.

"Why?" I ask. I could go to Pokey's. He'd let me in. His bedroom is on the ground floor. I could camp out in his closet. If I stay, she'll think everything's okay, and it will go back to normal, *our* normal.

Mama thinks for a minute. My hand rests on the latch to the door. The latch is sticky, as if Billy once touched it with jam on his hands.

"Why?" Mama repeats back. "Because I love you. Because you're my little girl." Her voice quavers on the word *little*. Billy looks scared now, his hands clasped together and his mouth tight.

"When you go away, we have to lie. We get scared. I nearly drowned!"

"What?" she asks, her hands flying to her face. She's alarmed, but she is also shielding herself from attack, as if my words are fragments of glass. "I wasn't gone that long. I left you food. My mother used to leave me alone all the time. It makes you strong."

"It makes you *scared*!" I shout, bursting into tears.

Billy just stares, like he can't believe sushi night turned into this crying fest.

"You don't know how good you've got it!" shouts Mama, her face reddening. She's probably wishing she had a bottle. Maybe she's trying to remember if she has one hidden somewhere in the cabin.

"I suppose I'm the sea witch in the story," says Mama, her face clouding over.

I am crying so hard that I am having trouble speaking. She looks at me, still angry, but also surprised. It's not the story she had expected.

"You're Annie," I say, barely audible. "The sea witch is your medicine."

I knew Grandma Lillian used to leave Mama alone. And Elizabeth used to leave Lillian. I've been hearing those stories all my life. A lot of hurt feelings, and girls left alone, and mothers who did the best they could. I wanted a different story.

I blow the air out of my cheeks and swipe the back of my hand under my eyes to wipe away the tears. The clock on the stove clacks, and a drop of water falls from the tap into the dishwater. Other than that, it is silent. Even Billy, for once, is quiet.

"Mama," I say. "Mr. Chadawack came by. The whale-watching place called about the job."

"Hmm," she says.

I worry now that I've cut the string that links our tin-can telephones. She will never talk to me again. She will be mad at me forever. She'll run away to the mainland, and next time she won't come back. And it will all be my fault. I should be upset, but now I am calm. I am just so, so tired. The tap drips again, the sound like the plink of a ukulele.

"Can you at least teach me to surf, for real?" I ask. "I want to win the next surf contest. Then I want to shove the trophy up Wendy Wishart's nose."

Billy barks a laugh, breaking the tension. Mama never needed surf lessons, so maybe she never thought about actually teaching me. There is a second or two of silence.

"That I can do," says Mama in a voice as tiny as a chickadee's teardrop.

I just nod. I can't talk anymore. My whole body is vibrating, as if I am catching a gigantic tidal wave. I consider still going to Pokey's, removing myself for a night. But I love waking up in the cabin when Mama is home and laughing and overcooking strips of bacon until they're the texture of luggage straps. I just love hearing her laugh. After she snorts, her laugh jangles, like the sound of a charm bracelet on a thin wrist, like the sound of eagles circling the woods, watching over their magic.

TUESDAY MORNING SURFING CLUB

At first I think I'm dreaming. Mama is standing over me, a big grin on her face and a glass in her hand. She's already in her wetsuit. It kind of makes her look like a Marvel superhero.

"Time to get up, Adelaide."

"What?" I ask. I'm surfacing from sleep, heading to the bubbles of reality above me. "I don't have school."

"But you have surf school," she says, thrusting the glass at me. It looks like it's filled with green fur, like she blended Oscar the Grouch. It reminds me of the loaf of bread I once found pushed to the back of the cupboard. It glowed with green mold.

"Drink this," she says, holding it under my nose. It smells like mown grass and seaweed. I must have been totally conked out. I can't believe she ran the blender without waking me.

"What is that?" I ask, wrinkling my nose. I want to trade it in for a banana smoothie.

"This is a Green Goblin, my own recipe. It makes you surf better."

"Not worth it," I say, throwing my pillow over my head. She grabs the pillow and tosses it on the floor.

"Surfers are like farmers. We get up early—if the surf is good. Shake a leg, Billy. You're coming too."

"I don't want to be a farmer," he groans. He never even changed into pajamas. We all fell into bed exhausted after all the upheaval.

"I'll go to the beach, but I'm not drinking that," I say, swinging my legs to the cabin floor. I said I wanted to learn to surf. Be careful what you wish for, they say. It's the first rule of fairy tales.

Billy and I flop around, looking for our gear. I finally find my wetsuit where I left it outside when Mrs. Polk dropped us off. I should have rinsed it with tap water. Billy starts struggling into his wetsuit, his eyes still only half-open. Billy is not a fan of mornings either.

"You should have rinsed that," says Mama, gesturing to my wetsuit right on cue. "I'll go get the sunscreen."

She pops back into the cabin, and I'm glad I don't have to be the one to remember everything. I hear the crunch of footsteps.

"Adelaide!" I hear.

It's Chadawack, looking red-faced and angry, his meaty hands clenched at his sides. He's wearing his green fleece and khaki shorts, as usual.

"Hi, Mr. Chadawack," I say, out of habit, the way you sing back a greeting to a teacher.

"I'm done waiting, Adelaide. I want my rent, last month and this month. I've got a lot of people waiting for this cabin, you know."

I nod. I resist pointing out that there really aren't any people waiting for this cabin because, unlike the ones he rents to tourists, it hasn't been updated in fifteen years and has a toilet that barely flushes. It doesn't appear on his website because it looks like what it is—run-down and faded, with a whiff of mold.

"You know, I can't say I've seen your mother around in days. Is she even here? I should call the authorities!"

Chadawack often talks about "the authorities" when we're late with rent or when he thinks Mama's letting us run wild. Just then Mama steps out of the cabin, a bottle of sunscreen in her hand.

"Who are we calling?" Mama asks. "The plumber about our dripping kitchen tap? I could have sworn all of us in Cedarveil were told to conserve water."

She glares at Chadawack. She has never been afraid of him and is not about to start.

"I'm here to see about the rent," he says, but takes a step back. Mama is intimidating when she's mad.

"Well, I put an envelope with a check through your mail slot last night, as it so happens. Should cover last month. The rest is on the way."

She pauses to allow this news to sink in with Chadawack, who looks slightly deflated. He seems to enjoy complaining about the late rent more than actually receiving it.

"If you'll excuse us, we've got some surfing to do. You should probably put on some of this," Mama says, pointing at him with the sunscreen. "You look a little red."

Chadawack nods grimly, his hands still clenched and his jaw set. I think I hear his teeth grind together.

"I'll go cash that check," he says. "If it clears, I'll call the plumber. My water bill is already sky high."

He grumbles the last part and heads off down the trail, his sandals crunching on the leaves.

"Let's bounce," says Mama, slapping her hand on her thigh. Mama doesn't have a middle speed—it's full steam ahead or serious chill. She's not a morning enthusiast unless surfing is involved. She takes a glug of the green drink.

"Ahh," she says to bug me. "So good."

I smile despite myself. We all tuck our boards under our arms and march toward the beach. Together. This time I've remembered to put on wetsuit booties. They leave prints in the wet trail. Billy keeps yawning as we walk. When we reach the beach, he plunks down on a log, sulking.

"You want to have the first go, Adelaide?" asks Mama.

I nod. I'm here, after all.

The sky is a smooth gray, and the waves are rolling in steady sets. Mama cocks her head and studies the waves, as if they are talking to her. We wade into the water, flop down on our boards and start paddling. I wonder what I could really do with more lessons and more work. I feel that I haven't scratched the surface. I feel that I haven't scratched *my* surface. A wave slops over my head, and I realize I had better pay attention.

"A good one is coming, Adelaide. Oh, it's gnarly," Mama shouts. Her hair is in two neat braids, the way I always picture her.

A good one is coming. Mama can feel it. I can feel it. She sees it rolling in and gestures for me to follow.

"Now! Adelaide, you got this!"

I see her looking at me with love, with expectation and then annoyance—I should go! I pop up too and steady my stance. I ride the wave in, then turn to see her watching me.

"That's my girl," she says, pumping her fist in the air.

I stagger onto the beach, holding my board. I can't help but grin. My heart is pounding but in a good way.

"Now me," says Billy, springing to his feet. He grabs his board and charges to the shore. Mama laughs at his sudden change of mind.

"Okay, grommet. There's waves for everyone today."

When Mama is happy, there is no one who shines brighter. Her eyes sparkle like beach glass, and she makes this snorting sound just before she laughs.

THE FIRST DAY OF SUMMER

A lot has happened over the past few weeks, so many things that, starting today, I'm writing them all down in a notebook. It's different putting my stories down on paper. It feels brave. Ms. Cranberg suggested it as a way to document my summer holidays. Plus, she told me flat out that I'm a talented writer and should "pursue" it. I had never even thought of that before—that I could be a writer or that anyone would be interested in what I have to say about anything.

But then Ms. Cranberg told me that one of my essays for class had been chosen to be read at the end-of-year school assembly. I could not believe it! The bad part is that I have to read it myself. Pokey has already heard me read it out loud three times. He says if I eat blowfish or something right before the assembly and get sick and can't go on, he will give the address for me. Which would be funny, because it's called "Mother, Daughter and the Perfect Wave." It's all about her teaching me to surf.

We've been getting up early and going to bed early. Every morning, if the surf is good, Mama and I go out together and catch a few waves. Sometimes Billy comes along, sometimes he stays in bed and sleeps until it's time to get ready for school. But Mama has been going to bed extra super early. I think it's because that makes her miss her medicine less. She may go back to it, I don't know. But for now, it's lights out at 9 p.m.

Bad news is that Mama was too late to get the job at the whale-watching station. Good news is that she landed a job working in the kitchen at guess where? The Wisharts' resort, Moon Over Water. Well, I guess it's only permanent if Mama can keep the job. And can stand working for the Wisharts.

They needed a prep cook in their kitchen, and she landed an interview—and was offered the job on the spot. Mama was so excited when she came home, carrying a greasy bag of fish and chips for our dinner to celebrate. I think we were all a little nervous that our good fortune was hitched to the Wishart wagon, but we Scratches have to take our breaks where we can get them.

"Marcia Wishart interviewed me herself in her office next to the kitchen. She looked at my résumé and said I was the only truly experienced cook who'd walked through her door that day." Mama had paused there, allowing herself a moment of pride while she unwrapped a bundle of fish and chips.

"You're a really good cook, Mama," I'd said, which was kind of funny, because we were having takeout at the time.

"After she offered me the job, she said something about you helping out Evie. That's nice, Adelaide. You're getting to be a big kid now. I love the way you look out for the little ones."

I'd just nodded, sinking my fork into the flaky hot fish. I was surprised Mrs. Wishart had found out about that, but people in Cedarveil talk. We'd all clinked mugs of milk and eaten until we were full, and it was a happy night.

The hard part for Mama is keeping a job, so we'll see how it goes. It's only been two weeks, but she's making enough money to keep Chadawack off our backs for now. It sucks having to deal with him, but the trade-off is being so close to the beach. And it's hard to find affordable places to live in Cedarveil because the mainland people keep buying up property for their summer homes.

I'm kind of sad that school is ending, I always am, but I've almost made enough money at the library to pay for the Red Cross babysitting course. Pokey is going to take it with me, and Mama says if she keeps up with the job at the resort, regular and steady, there'll be enough money for soccer or basketball camp for me and Billy. I go to sleep with my fingers crossed, and every day that I wake up and she is there, making her horrifying Green Goblin drink, I am happy. And I am getting better at duck diving.

And guess what? Grandma Lillian is coming for a visit just after school ends. She's going to rent one of the other cabins for a spell and hang out with us while Mama works her evening shifts so we won't be alone. There will be another adult to help us—and Mama. It could be a total disaster. We haven't seen Grandma Lillian much in recent years, and both of them have tempers. Mama says Lillian can tell me stories about when Mama was a girl, and even from when Lillian herself was a girl. There is so much I want to know.

And now I also have a secret dream. A dream I'll write down in this notebook, but I haven't even told Pokey. I want to surf in Australia, on Bondi Beach, where Nick and Jeanie met. I want to see the sharks and kangaroos and parrots and spiders one day. And I want to make enough money babysitting this summer to buy a new bike.

I want to enter the Belle of the Board surf contest again, and I want to do better. Okay, I actually want to win, but I'll settle for at least not making a fool of myself. I want to remember that I want all these things in case the cabin gets dark and cold and lonely. I want to stop worrying about Mama leaving again when she's still right here, her rubber boots by the door.

I am afraid she will leave again. I am afraid she will drink again. I am afraid she will lose her temper and then her job. I can see how much her eyes shine and her back straightens when she has a regular job. Mama loves to work, despite her track record.

I have only three more days before I give my speech. I might stumble over my words. The other kids might laugh at my story. All I can do is practice and hope for the best. After the surf contest, I thought I was done trying. With everything. I guess that was a lie, or at least I've changed my mind. But guess what again? Mama said she would book off work and that she would be there, right at 2 p.m. when the assembly begins. She even offered to bring her old Super 8 video camera to film it—an idea I vetoed. I was secretly happy that she was so excited. Ms. Cranberg says I just have to picture myself doing well—visualize success.

Now that I've written one story, I have another kind of hunger. I want to finish the story about the sea witch with the bitter gold eyes and the lonely girl, Annie. I want to write about a loyal friend who shares his food and keeps secrets. I can imagine filling all these pages.

I picture a girl who survived being left alone, even if she was scared. A girl who's starting to realize that she comes from a long line of survivors, that it might be in her blood, like long legs, like salt water, like the sound of the surf.

ACKNOWLEDGMENTS

I would like to thank Orca Book Publishers for believing in this story and for making it better each step of the way as it became a book. My gratitude to the Orca pod, including Ruth Linka, Andrew Wooldridge, Olivia Gutjahr, editor extraordinaire Sarah Howden and copyeditor Vivian Sinclair. Thank you to Liam for lending some surfing expertise—any blunders in terms or technique are mine alone. My appreciation to Sophie Dubé for the cover art.

I would also like to acknowledge the support of my dynamo of an agent, Kerry Sparks, of Levine Greenberg Rostan. I hope we have many more exciting creative projects in our future.

This story began with the idea of exploring a relationship in which someone important in your life makes it very difficult to love them. While the story of Adelaide Scratch is fictional, the home children referenced in the book were a real phenomenon. Between 1869 and 1932, over 100,000 children migrated to Canada from Great Britain, with many working as farm laborers. There are several books on this subject, including *Marjorie Too Afraid to Cry: A Home Child Experience* by Patricia Skidmore, which I consulted.

Victoria-based playwright Joan MacLeod also wrote a moving play about the child-migration scheme, titled *Homechild*, which I had the good fortune to see.

My thanks to my family, including my father, Ron Manzer; Marjorie and Barrie Leach; my husband, David; and my two surfers, A.J. and Briar. And a shout-out to our dog, Cedar, who, honestly, doesn't really care if I write books but does enjoy sleeping under my feet when I'm at the computer.

I would like to also honor the memory of two special people who were fiercely loved and are deeply missed: my aunt Carolyn McMullen and my friend Karen Kobayashi. As always, I express my gratitude for my mother, Kathryn, and my sister, Patricia, whom I miss every day and who are always in my thoughts.

And, finally, thank you to all the librarians and teachers, like Ms. Cranberg in the story, who—despite steep obstacles—support kids, all kids, in seeking out stories to learn about themselves and the world. Your work makes a difference, every day.

Jenny Manzer is the author of *Save Me, Kurt Cobain* and *My Life as a Diamond*, which was shortlisted for numerous awards, including the Diamond Willow Award, Chocolate Lily Award, Victoria Children's Book Prize and the Silver Birch Award. She has a degree in creative writing and was a finalist for the 2013 CBC Creative Nonfiction Prize, one of Canada's most prestigious literary competitions. She lives with her family in Victoria, British Columbia.

MORE OF ORCA'S MIDDLE-GRADE FICTION

"This coming-of-age story examines issues that are relatable to many Muslim readers...A wholesome story with room and grace for all the characters to learn and grow."
—*Kirkus Reviews*

"A...realistic story that explores bullying and its effects...while offering fascinating information about African Grey parrots."
—*Booklist*

★ "Wonderfully whimsical and positively poignant."
—*Booklist*

"This well-paced, rather disturbing, and very creepy collection will appeal to a wide variety of readers."
—*Kirkus Reviews*

MORE BY JENNY MANZER

Live as your true self, no matter the cost.

"An engaging sports story."
—*Kirkus Reviews*

"Competition between teams is fierce, as is camaraderie within the team."
—*Booklist*